Shetland Black

Shetland Black

Laureen Johnson

Notes: The story takes place in the 1990s. The places, the characters and the events are all entirely fictional.

The title: *Shetland Black* — darkest of the natural colours of Shetland wool.

Shetland Black

ISBN 1 898852 87 1

First published by The Shetland Times Ltd, 2002.

British Library Cataloguing-in-Publication Data.
A catalogue record for this book is available from the British Library.

Cover illustration by and copyright of:
Jeanette Nowak.

Printed and published by
The Shetland Times Ltd.,
Gremista,
Lerwick,
Shetland. ZE1 0EP

For Isobel and Jamie

Contents

Acknowledgments

For their help and advice, I would like to thank:

Mr Graeme Couper
Inspector Arnold Duncan
and the late nurse Mary Wood

Any mistakes are mine, not theirs.

My thanks also to everyone who has encouraged me towards the completion and publishing of this book.

Shetland Black

Characters

In Whalvoe:

Meg Inkster
Mary and Donald Jamieson
Willie Hendry   -   Mary's brother
Eric Hendry   -   Willie's son
Cissie Hendry   -   Mother of Mary, Willie and John
Jack and Marilyn Thompson

Outwith Whalvoe:

John and Mina   -   Willie's brother and sister-in-law
Gail and Stewart   -   Willie's daughter and boyfriend
Joanne and Chris   -   Mary and Donald's daughters

Amy   -   friend of Marilyn's
Bob Tulloch   -   local publican
Evan Ritchie   -   friend of Meg's
Gordon and Jacqueline -   friends of Jack and Marilyn
Hamish   -   friend of Eric's
Jessie Anderson   -   friend of Cissie's
Nessie Clark   -   caretaker of the camping böd

Sergeant Fraser
Doctor Macintyre
Two policemen

Brugafirth folk we meet in passing:

Sandy the postman, Annie Brown and Christine who work in the Brugafirth shop, Kathy Bruce the barmaid, Tom at the garage, Charlie Henderson; pubgoers Andrew, Jim o Braeview, Tammie Sinclair, Old Jeemie, Alastair and Maurice; shop customers Erty, Bessie and Janette.

Map of Whalvoe

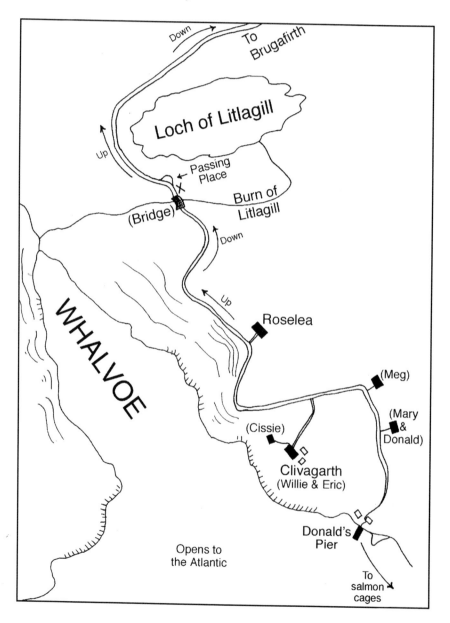

Shetland Black

Chapter 1

Meg

Slaughter.

Innocent victim.

How do you feel... Babble.

Coherence. *Pursuing a line of enquiry... and now ... weather... Phil Miles.*

Babble babble *spring. April sunshine ... England sixteen degrees...*

The weather forecast crystallised out of indignation. England sixteen degrees! Did he ever mention Scotland, let alone Shetland?

Meg Inkster jerked fully awake. Radio Two declared it to be seven-oh-five. She'd slept in. The radio wasn't loud enough. She must have moved the volume control last night without noticing.

She had ten minutes to get to her post office to meet the mail van from Lerwick, bringing the day's mailbags for sorting and delivery. She had three miles to drive on a narrow twisting road. And it was raining. Damn Phil Miles and his London complacency.

Clothes on. Speed wash. Thank God for perms.

The Rayburn in the kitchen was warm, but there was no time to tend the fire. The house would be cold at night. Must try to get home at dinner-time. Not easy, might still be short-handed in the shop today. Maybe Mary would nip across and see to the fire. Phone her later.

Next winter, she resolved for the tenth time, hauling on her jacket, she would have oil or electric central heating. Something that didn't need a resident stoker. If she was still in this house.

The car needed persuading to start, of course. Didn't like rainy mornings. Another thing it would be nice to have was a garage, like Mary's.

1

She backed down and out on to the road, not bothering to look for traffic. At seven in the morning she rarely saw another car on the Whalvoe road. There were only four other inhabited houses. It was too early for either Donald or Mary to be driving. In another couple of weeks, once the lambing was under way, Willie Hendry might be on the rounds of his various holdings, but today his pick-up truck was safely parked down by the Clivagarth gable. Just as well. Willie was notoriously short-sighted, and meeting him on this road could be hair-raising. It was equally hair-raising to meet his eighteen-year-old son Eric, still at the rally-driving stage. But Eric's blue hatchback, too, was still safely at home.

The rain was fairly lashing down and the car was cold. Meg shivered.

Slaughter. Innocent victim.

What had put that in her head?

Pursuing a line of enquiry.

Something unpleasant at the back of her mind. It must have been a story on the radio. Or had she dreamed it?

She turned on Radio Scotland, but the news was over, and there seemed to be nothing but politics. Maybe it had happened in England. Some maniac with a shotgun, perhaps. It had been something horrible like that. Down south.

She fairly flew around the first sharp bend, and past the Roselea drive. The Audi was away; Jack Thompson was on night shift. Marilyn and the baby were alone in the palace.

Palace? *Gettin siccar, Meg, in dee old age.* But Roselea *was* a palace of a house, dominating in its size and newness. And Marilyn did tend only to patronise Meg's shop for papers and petrol. She was a supermarket shopper. Like a few others. Meg sighed.

Maybe the mail van would be late today too, not waiting officiously. Maybe Christine, her best Saturday shop assistant, would be back at work today. Maybe Donald wouldn't sneak in again at six o'clock to try to buy drink. If he did, she'd show him the door this time. He'd go straight to the pub anyway, but at least she could still look Mary in the eye.

Maybe it wouldn't be a bad day after all.

She swung round the second sharp bend and started down towards the burn of Litlagill.

There was something bright yellow by the side of the road, on the corner beyond the bridge. Slightly down over the banking, towards the burn.

Plastic. Bloody plastic bags. They blew everywhere. And did anybody ever bother to pick them up?

Damn this rain. The wipers could hardly cope.

It wasn't a plastic bag. Maybe something had fallen off Willie Hendry's pick-up on the corner. She stopped the car and wound down the streaming window.

There seemed to be no sound, anywhere in the whole valley. The car door opened and shut silently, her feet fell silent on tarmac stone, there was no sound at all. And no feeling, except cold.

The bright yellow colour was a jacket. It was a body by the side of the road. A slight young man, a stranger, with his head among stones.

Shetland Black

Chapter 2

Cissie

Cissie Hendry eyed the rain in annoyance as she sipped her morning tea. She really wanted to get outside today. Start clearing up and digging the still winter-bound garden. Go for a walk round the banks. Anything. She was stiffening up in here. So little to do. Didn't even have to carry in peats any more.

It was splendid, though, there was no denying it, to have a warm house at the touch of a button. She would miss the sunny space of the peat hill, the laverock song, the voar breeze on your face, the jokes and the gossip… But she wouldn't miss the toil of it, the strain on the back and the sore arthritic shoulder. And it wasn't always so sociable, either, with fewer hands to be found now, and Thelma gone.

Not like it used to be, when Cissie was young, with eight in the family, and cousins next door, plenty of young folk to raise and turn and take the peats home. It had all been chatter and horse-play, with Mam to chide and Faider to laugh and join in. Such fun. Such youth. Such a long time ago.

She'd better defrost the deep freeze. The ice was building up round the lid.

There was a flurry and a barking of dogs outside, and Willie appeared through the rain on the path between their two houses.

It was barely nine o'clock. Had something happened to Eric with yon old car?

She was at the door to meet him. "Willie? What's pitten dee ower dis early?"

He came in, quiet as usual, and sat down, thus compelling her to sit too.

"Du'll no be surprised, Mam, but Robert is just phoned fae Leith. Babsy passed awey apo da night."

Cissie sat straight, eyes on her son.

"So dan. She's awa."

Willie looked out the window. "Da funeral'll be on Tuesday, he towt."

They sat in silence.

"Will du be aa right?" he said awkwardly.

Cissie rose, grasping her empty cup, and carried it to the sink.

"I'll be aa right! She wis me sister, but she wis a body o eighty in poor helt. Naebody lests for ever, my joy, an come ta my day o life, I'm seen ower muckle ta set me doon an gie in ta dis. Never du worry aboot me. Is du telled Mary, an John?"

"I phoned dem eenoo. Mary said she wid be doon ta see dee later on trow da day. I tink John'll be comin ower da night."

Cissie was rinsing out her cup. "Poor soul Mary, she doesna hae her sorrows ta seek eenoo. Does du ken whan Donald cam hame da streen?"

"Mam," said Willie quietly, "du soodna be watchin."

"Deil een o me wis watchin! I hed ta rise an tak a tablet, an da van lights guid up ta da hoose as I stöd apo da stairhead. It wis twenty past wan. An dat wis laekly him fae taytime."

"Donald haes a lock on eenoo. Dey're surely gyaain ta tak ower his salmon fairm."

Cissie's cup rattled back upon the cup rack, dry. "Da best at could happen. Aa yon debts! Da very best at could happen! Aless at he'll laekly drink whatever money might be made."

Willie rose. "Weel, Mam, I'll hae ta geng. I hae feeding ta fetch."

Cissie looked at him. He was tall and gaunt and greying. He was lifeless.

"Du'll no be gyaain ta da funeral," she said, sounding certain.

"Na. I'm hed enough o funerals."

Poor Willie. She stepped after him, unable to touch him.

He turned.

"Du's da last wan noo, Mam."

Did he have to say that?

"Yea," she said, "dat am I. Aless maybe for Davie — but dat we'll never ken."

The door closed.

Cissie stood very still, and looked out the window through the rain. She was still standing in the same place long after Willie's pick-up went up the Clivagarth road and headed away to Lerwick.

Shetland Black

----------------------------------- Chapter 3 -----------------------------------

Marilyn

Marilyn Thompson closed the bedroom door behind her and summoned a smile for the peerie stalwart in the baby-walker.

"Shush, Martin." She steered him down the passage. "Daddy's goin ta sleep."

She shut the kitchen door, turned on the radio so low she could barely hear it, and reached for her cigarettes. Perched at the breakfast bar, she looked out over the road and a grey sweep of Whalvoe. Rain obscured the distant headlands and the tops of the hills on the other side of the voe. Their precious view. Glass box.

In about half an hour she would drive to Amy's in Scalloway and spend most of the day. She'd wait till Jack fell asleep first. Shouldn't go till then.

It wasn't her fault he was crabbit again. She couldn't go back to bed with him now. Martin was on the go.

Martin was always on the go. Always moving, always active, always investigating. He slept twelve hours at night with the same concentrated intensity, but the day was demanding, and long. Especially when he had to be kept quiet so Jack could sleep. It was much easier to take him out.

She inhaled deeply, and watched her son getting to grips with a car magazine.

So there was a lot of uncertainty at Sullom Voe. Wondering whose job would be next for the chop. And the mortgage was hanging over him. She knew all that. He'd been on about it months ago.

"So sell da hoose," she'd said. "I hate bidin here anywye."

Such a row they'd had, all why didn't this and that, and if only and so on. She'd have been better off lying. Too honest. It didn't pay.

The car magazine was suffering. Marilyn removed it from Martin's determined hands and substituted a mail order sale list. She never saw anything worth buying in a sale list. Sale goods were just what nobody wanted the first time.

She'd have to cut back on clothes, Jack had said when they had the last bank statement. He didn't know how mortifying it was not to be able to get back into her favourite outfits. Martin was nearly a year old now. Perhaps she should have breast-fed him, however painful it was. People said the weight just fell away.

She needed her hair done. What a sight she looked now. If she were to walk back into the Royal Hotel, the receptionist who took her place would hide a smile, sly sculptured bitch that she was.

Maybe she needed a holiday, away from here. Jack might agree. He liked the sun. Maybe they could leave Martin with Mam.

Maybe what she really needed was to get back to work. Part-time would be fine. Maybe Amy . . .?

Whatever she needed, last night had been a mistake. No, more than that, a disaster. A stupid idea, best forgotten.

The rain had stopped. Thank God.

She stubbed out her cigarette, and began to change Martin, and dress him for visiting.

They left Roselea quietly.

She'd stop in Brugafirth for petrol. Meg Inkster had recently installed a self-service system. For a peerie country shop, Meg's was quite advanced. She ought to have a better look round sometime.

There were cars coming and going, and a group of people standing outside the shop door as Marilyn filled the Audi. There were no smiles. Heads were shaking, voices hushed. Some bad news.

She spied an acquaintance of Jack's, and said hello as she passed. He stepped towards her.

"Weel," he said, "you widna a been at da pub da streen, laekly."

She looked from him to his companion.

"No. Are we missed onything? I saw da police car staandin dere. What's been happenin?"

"You're no heard? Dey wir a camper fellow ida pub da streen an Meg fan him dead at da brig o Litlagill dis moarnin."

"Dead? What wis happened him?"

"Wha kens? Edder he fell an hat his head, or he spewed an shockit. He wis hed a braa guid dram, dey say. Da remains is gyaain ta Aberdeen for a post-mortem."

"Or of coorse," said the other man half-knowingly, "he might a been hitten be a car."

The group of people seemed to have drifted away. A chill wind swirled around the empty forecourt.

"Did you say he wis a camper?"

"He wis bidin ida campin böd. Nessie Clark is hed ta geng an identify da boady. Dey're no wun in yet ta fin his gaer. Da key wisna on him. Da police is gyaain ta pick up a key fae da Tourist Office."

Her face was white, she knew it was. She opened her mouth to speak.

"An dat's anidder thing," said the half-knowing man. "If dat's whaar he wis bidin, what wis he doin half a mile in da rodd ta Whalvoe?"

What she said was "It's an awful thing."

The shop radio was tuned to SIBC. There was no sign of Meg. A tall lass with dyed blonde hair served Marilyn, telling the previous customer that Meg was in the office.

"She's haein a braa moarnin. Police statements, an aa yon kerry-on. An folk keeps phonin."

A news bulletin was saying something about an accident in the Kames. Then came the story of the body by the burn. Believed to be a New Zealander, early twenties, five foot ten, slight growth of beard. Anyone who might have information regarding this man, or who had seen or spoken to him during the day or evening of the thirteenth, was asked to get in touch with the police.

Lonely in the car outside, baby Martin began to cry.

Shetland Black

———————— **Chapter 4** ————————

Donald

Donald Jamieson awoke from a blackness of sleep and realised it was half past ten. He lay still, breathing evenly, aware of a vague ache behind his eyes. He really must get an eyesight test. Eye strain made your head sore. Poor focusing lately, middle age, bound to happen. Going to need glasses, likely.

The washing machine in the utility room below thudded into spin. He looked at the empty chair beside the bed. Mary had taken everything he'd been wearing yesterday. Cleaning fanatic, that woman. Better get up and away out of her road.

He rose slowly and searched for clothes. Stiff this morning, boy. Arthritis will set in before long. What could you expect, working at the cages so much, damp weather, oilskins all the time, condensation.

Good laugh at the pub last night. Tammie Sinclair was in good trim. Jim o Braeview too. Spoke to that New Zealand fellow. Yellow jacket.

Hood right up over his head. No, no, that wasn't right. That must have been in the afternoon.

The side door opened and shut. Mary had gone to the clothes-line. From the looks of the sky, it might not be dry for long. Go downstairs now and off down the road to the fish. No need to bother her making breakfasts. Just call out and say *see you at dinner-time.*

Young Eric was hosing down his car at the side of the Clivagarth barn. The post van was parked near by. The driver was talking to Cissie Hendry at her door.

Ought to meet the post. Might have a letter from the big shots today. *Welcome to the team. Glad to have you join us.* About time, too. The salmon business wasn't easy on a small scale. Everybody knew that. No shame in selling out to a big company. Sensible thing to do. And they'd still need a man on the spot to do the work. They'd still need him. Nothing surer.

Eric was getting into his car. He wasn't waiting for the post.

Donald came downstairs, went to the bathroom, then headed quietly out the side porch door, picking up his jacket. He called cheerio to Mary, and stood at the roadside waiting for the approaching post van.

Sandy the postman leaned across and opened the window. He brought a council tax bill. And news. His eyes were sharp with news.

The red van drew away.

Donald turned around and headed for his own van, parked at the far side of the turning area in front of the garage. He brought up short.

There was a dent in his left wing.

Mary, wash-basket in hand, reached him at that moment.

He looked at her, terrified.

---------------------------- **Chapter 5** ----------------------------

Eric

T he post van had followed the blue hatchback up the Clivagarth road. As Eric drove away towards Brugafirth, he could see in his rear-view mirror the red van turning in the opposite direction. He'd managed to avoid the postman.

He didn't want to hear the story from Sandy. There was a radio news bulletin still ringing in his ears. He could imagine the rumours flying already. More food for the bloody grapevine. Strong meat this time.

Eric drove fast. There was never any traffic. Must get off this narrow road. Might meet Dad on his way home from Lerwick. First meeting of the day. Might have to stop, and Dad would wind down the window and ask questions.

They often communicated through car windows. Or left each other notes in the empty house.

No car at Roselea.

Round the bend before the Litlagill burn. There's the place. A couple of cars parked, folk looking around. Sight-seers. Bloody hyenas. Smelling blood. Sniffing around.

A sheep ran straight across the road ahead. Eric stood on the brakes and the car sledged onto the stony hard shoulder. Cursing, he edged back onto the tarmac and accelerated away, with alerted recognising eyes now following him. Eyes everywhere. Everywhere you went, everything you did, all noticed. No privacy. Roll on September and city anonymity.

He reached the main road junction at Brugafirth and had to wait a moment for passing traffic. He ought to listen to some proper music. He looked down at his tapes.

A key.

On the floor below the glove compartment lay a key. It must have slid out from under the seat when he braked. It was a large, old-fashioned key, on a keyring, with an attached tag reading *The Böd, Brugafirth. Please return to Tourist Office, Lerwick.*

Eric held on tightly to the steering-wheel. His body was shaking.

Shetland Black

Chapter 6

Phone Calls

"Hello?"

"Hello, is that you, Willie? Sergeant Fraser here."

"Oh. And what can I do for you, Sergeant?"

"Is young Eric at home, Willie? I wondered if I might have a word with him?"

"He's no home at da moment."

"Do you know when he'll be back, by any chance?"

"I couldna say. What were you wantin him for, Sergeant? Can I tak a message?"

"Oh well, it's just that we're making a few enquiries, you know, about the camper. You'll have heard about him, the New Zealand fellow that was found dead?"

"My midder is just been tellin me. Awful thing. But...."

"We're just asking around anybody who might have spoken to him or seen him last night, folk that were in the pub and so on. Now Eric wasn't in the pub last night, I believe. But his car was parked fairly late on at the passing-place up by the bridge there, where the body was found."

"Oh."

"And we wondered, you see, if he'd seen the man around when he came back to his car. Do you know what time he got home?"

"Oh, I couldna say."

"Anyway, maybe you could ask him to give me a ring when he comes in?"

"I'll do dat."

"I don't suppose you saw the fellow yourself, Willie? He wouldn't have been around Whalvoe any time during the day? Young chap, fairly tall, bright yellow jacket?"

"Dat might a been him at guid walkin oot aroond da Ness efter denner-time."

"That was very likely him. Did you speak to him?"

"No, no, I wis doon ida sooth park feedin da sheep. I just saw him getting oot o a car abön Donald's salmon pier."

"Oh, did you know the car, Willie?"

"Weel, I tink it wis Jack Thompson. He wis laekly geen him a lift in da rodd."

"Oh yes. Well, Willie, thanks for your help."

*   *   *   *   *   *

"Hello, can I spaek ta Meg, please? Tell her it's Mary Jamieson."
. . . "Hello, Mary?"

"Meg. It's me. Could du tak me hame tree pints o mylk? I dönna hae time ta come ta da shop dis efternön."

"OK, I'll do dat. Er — foo are you da day?"

"Oh, er — aa right. Donald is awa doon wirkin wi da fish an I'm started spring-cleanin."

"Well, good for dee."

"An du's surely hed some day, I'm hearin."

"It wisna very fine. But it's aa back ta normal noo. Da only budder is haein ta repeat da story sae aften."

"Are dey ony mair news? Are dey fun oot wha he is yet?"

"Yes, we're just hed Nessie Clark alang wis, her at looks efter da Böd, du kens. Dey hed ta fetch her oot dis moarnin ta identify da boady, poor sowl. I tink it's geen her a braa shak. Weel, she can tell wis at da police is come wi a key — du kent at dey couldna fin da key o da Böd? Onywye, dey're wun in noo, an dey're taen awa his papers an aa his gaer an surely gyaain ta mak contact wi his fock."

"He wis just a young man, wisn' he?"

"Twenty-two, Nessie said."

"Just a boy!"

"No muckle idder as Eric. Slight-biggit, laek Eric."

"It's terrible!"

"His name wis Terry Pearson. Oh — an Mary, da police is surely gyaain aroond spaekin ta folk at wis at da pub da streen, because dis boy wis dere for a while. So dey'll maybe be aside Donald among da rest, I hear."

"Oh dear God . . . Meg, does du tink . . . did . . . what . . . what are dey sayin happened tae him?"

"Weel, I dönna tink onybody can say what happened tae him till dey get da results o da post-mortem."

"No, of coorse. But what are dey *tinkin?*"

"Noo, Mary, du kens as weel as me. Some tinks wan thing, some anidder. But if du's axin me what *I* tink, all at I can say is what I'm been sayin aa day. He wis lyin wi his head alang a muckle stane, doon ower da broo o da rodd. It wis a dark night, an he laekly wisna very steady on his feet. He could aesy just a faan."

"Oh Meg."

"Dat's what *I* saw, Mary. Nae mair as dat."

"What ta da deevil wis he *doin* yonder? He never sood a been at Litlagill!"

"Oh weel, dere again, wha kens. I doot he just guid da wrang wye ida dark. Mary, I doot I'll hae ta go. Keep du on wi dee cleanin an I'll nip ower wi dee mylk efter tay. Der some tablets come here fae da surgery for dee midder, but I can geng doon alang her wi dem as I come hame."

"Oh, she'll be blyde ta see dee. She got her hidmast sister's death news dis moarnin. I'm just gyaain doon ta see her shortly."

"Oh less, poor Cissie. Der always something, aren' dey?"

Shetland Black

—————————— Chapter 7 ——————————

Meg, Saturday Teatime

Meg turned down the Clivagarth road with reluctance. She was late home as it was.

She must have seen them all today. All the regular customers from Brugafirth and Houbister, and a good many rarities. Accidental death was good for business, a cynic might say.

Ach, the folk were interested. Was that surprising?

There had been shock in Brugafirth this morning. Sympathy for herself too, some from unexpected quarters. Concern for the dead man —dead boy, as they all thought of him. And then, curiosity about him.

Information was now on the rounds, and in the shop they had heard several rounds by closing time. Nothing was reliable unless it had come from a very dependable first-hand source. Anything else was disclaimed as hearsay, but it got passed on just the same. Anyone who knew anything had been asked: Nessie Clark, Meg's own shop assistants, Bob from the pub and all the pub-goers from last night. Except Donald. He'd been drinking till closing-time. No-one had seen Donald today.

No-one seemed to have phoned him either. Brugafirth knew Donald's movements last night better than he did himself, by all accounts. Nobody knew what to say to him.

Meg was beginning to feel bone-weary. And she hadn't had the heart to ask Mary to put her fire on.

Cissie was at the door to meet her.

"Meg, lass, come in. It's awful guid o dee ta come alang wi me tablets. It's an awful budder apo dee."

"No hit, Cissie, I'm comin by da head o da rodd onywye. Hit's nae budder at all. Foo are you?"

Cissie seemed not to have heard. She was opening the kitchen door.

"Noo, Meg, du'll just come in here an hae dee tay wi me."

This was a ritual they sometimes went through, the persuading and the declining, the "too much budder apo you, Cissie," and the "nonsense, lass, I'm blyde ta hae dee." They went through it again.

The kitchen was warm and inviting. Meg looked at the bone china cups, the neat slices of meat and cheese and the new-made bannocks, and sank into the nearest armchair. Cissie would want her share of the news too. Once more through the story wouldn't hurt. And Cissie might be in need of company tonight, poor body.

They worked their way through the normal small talk, but by the time the second cup of tea was poured, Meg had related the story of the camper.

Cissie shook her head. "Du most a gotten a braa gluff."

"I did dat."

The weathered face was kind, the eyes gentle.

"I canna get him oot o me mind."

Cissie nodded. "Du's no ta lat it lie in wi dee. He wis lang past dy help, an du did everything onybody could a done for him, poor object."

From next door, dogs began to bark.

"Foo wis Mary when she spak ta dee, Meg?"

"She seemed braaly upset."

"She wis da sam in here. Face laek a sheet. Aye lookin oot da window, keepin an eye on da rodd."

"I see."

"I don't tink he's been far da day, though. He guid sooth ower ta da fish for a start, dat's been aa. But she wis lippenin da police alang."

"Dey're been spaekin ta folk at wis in da pub da streen."

Cissie drained her teacup. "Yes, I ken. An she wis braaly fairt."

Meg said nothing.

"Donald cam hame at twenty past wan," said Cissie.

"He most a come straight fae da pub dan, wi what dey say."

"An did dey say what state he wis in?"

"Braaly weel on, I doot."

Cissie shook her head, her face grave. "I towt nae idder. What's da folk sayin aboot it, Meg?"

"Weel, everybody is just hoopin at da boy fell an hat his head. An hit might weel be da case. Dey were nae muckle obvious injury at all, nae brokken limbs or onything laek dat."

Through the window, they both saw the police car come along the high road and turn down to Clivagarth.

"It's aa right, Cissie," said Meg. "Eric wis maybe alang da pub da streen tö. He'll hae ta be seen alang wi da rest."

"Oh guid kens whaar he wis. I doot he wis farder afield. I heard da car comin hame aboot tree o'clock."

They looked at each other. The kitchen clock ticked.

"Do dey hae ony idea, Meg, whan death took place?"

Meg hesitated. "Dey seem ta say it wis maist laekly atween twal an two."

The face slackened a little. Meg looked momentarily out the window. She hadn't heard that from either policemen or doctor.

Cissie was still looking at her. "If da boady wid a been lyin dere at tree o'clock, wid Eric no a seen him?"

Easier question. "Weel, it's still braaly dark at tree o'clock, an it wis a night o rain. I tink onyeen comin *in* da rodd wid a missed him. He wis lyin doon ower da broo, a peerie bit dis side o da passing-place, just efter da brig. You really needed ta be comin oot fae Whalvoe tae a seen him. Especially ida dark."

A nod, then silence.

"Cissie," said Meg, "I wis sorry ta hear aboot your sister."

Cissie looked briefly at her plate. "She's no been weel for a while. I kent it wis comin."

Meg leaned forward a little, nodding.

"So it's just me at's left noo. Wan o wis oot o eight."

"I ken."

A moment of quiet.

Cissie lifted her head. "Still, it's just da wye o life. An I'm blyde I wan ta see her last year when she wis still ower weel."

"Hit's been a queer day, wan wye an anidder," said Meg.

"Hit's truly been dat. But does du ken, Meg, hit's aa queer days in Clivagarth noo, withoot Thelma. Dis is ten mont geen by noo, an you can hardly get a wird oot o Willie yet, an poor ting Eric, I tink dat ill aboot him athoot his midder. I sometimes winder if him an his faider says half a dizzen wirds ta een anidder ida coorse o a day."

18

"Do dey no get on, dan?"

"Oh, dey get on aa right. But da wan never seems ta ken anything aboot what da idder een is doin or tinkin or onything ava. I tink it widna be sae ill if Gail wis still hame, but she's in Brae aside da boyfreend, an no laekly ta come back. Eric just canna wait ta win awey sooth, an I canna blame him!"

The hands gripped tightly to the empty china cup.

"Babsy wis eighty year aald, an hed her life. Thelma wis only forty-tree."

"I ken."

Cissie sat up. "It's a queer thing, Meg, but da day I just canna keep fae tinkin aboot wir Davie. Du'll no ken wha dat wis?

"No."

"He wis da second aaldest een o wir faimily. Ten year aalder as me. I mind him fine. He jamp ship in New Zealand when I wis nine, an we never heard o him ageen."

"Never at all?"

"Never at all. Dey wir a rumour at someen cam hame wi a year or twa later at someen wis seen him, but we never heard anidder wird."

"Dey wir a lock o dat at guid on, dey say."

"Oh yea, but usually dey wrat hame efter a while. Mam lippened a letter in years."

The eyes were far away. Cissie was nine, ten, thirteen, waiting for the mail. The family stood round her, waiting, waiting. Shadows on the mind.

Meg rose and came to her side. "What's pitten him in your mind da day?"

"Oh, I dönna ken." The head shook a little. "Maybe I windered if he wisna still somewye apo dis eart, an I widna be da last wan. An dan, du sees, I towt, just laek we aa towt afore, at maybe something happened tae him, just laek dis poor boy at du fan dis moarnin. Dat wis what Faider aye towt. He couldna hae it ta be at Davie widna a written ta wis."

"Maybe he wis right."

There were tears now. Meg put an arm around the staunch shoulders. The smooth grey hair smelt of apples.

"It most a been hard for you aa."

Cissie reached for her hanky and blew her nose.

"Weel, it wis. Babsy wis dat tirn apon him, she never mentioned his name again, aless ta lay oot for him. Things wis aye awful black an white wi Babsy. Guid forgie me but it's true. Nane o her faimily wis ever supposed ta dö onything wrang. I aye tink wir Mary is laek her. Never spaeks aboot things. Never laeks admittin tae a faat. Keeps it all quiet."

"Noo, noo."

"Weel, she tells me nothing. Ower prood. Does she really tink at I dönna ken foo muckle Donald is drinkin? Does she tink at I'm no hearin it, when every sowl in Brugafirt can tell me?"

"Maybe," said Meg, "Mary just canna *bear* ta spaek aboot it."

"Oh, du's maybe right!" Cissie looked up, easily chastened. "I'm maybe bein ower hard apon her."

They rose to clear the table, and Meg washed up. She judged the moment to say "Weel, Cissie, tanks ta you for da tay, but I will hae ta be goin noo."

"Weel, lass, guid bliss dee for comin alang. Sometimes, du kens, you need someen ta spaek tae. I miss Thelma."

"I doot everyeen misses her."

They reached the door.

Cissie said "I tink apo yon poor midder in New Zealand da night. Whaar did he come fae, da boy?"

"Wellington, Nessie said. His name wis Terry Pearson. I axed if he hed ony Shetland connection, but naebody seemed ta ken."

Cissie laid a clutching hand on her arm. "Wellington?"

"Yes."

"An his name wis *Pearson* ?"

Cissie leaned against the porch wall.

"My name wis Pearson. Davie jamp ship in Wellington. Na, na, surely, it couldna be . . ."

Shetland Black

Chapter 8

Willie

Willie Hendry sat in the armchair by the Rayburn and watched the two at the table. The boy was polite to the policeman, the face attentive, the tone of voice steady, his hands clasped together in his lap. The interview wouldn't take long. It was just a formality.

He couldn't remember when he had last seen Eric sitting so still. The boy was always rushing off, always going somewhere. Half the time, Willie had no idea where. Pals, he thought. Hamish in Brugafirth, Derek in Tingwall, Colin and Richard in Lerwick. Football matches, discos and pubs at the weekend.

Did he have a girlfriend? Willie didn't think so. But he might be wrong.

If the policeman, or anybody, was suddenly to ask Willie searching questions about his son's life, Willie would have precious few answers. Eric was going to Edinburgh University in September to study engineering. He was working meantime as a builder's labourer with Henry Mann in Brugafirth. He passed his test in January. He hates sheep. He doesn't say much.

Eric had not explained to Willie where he was last night. It had been a bit awkward, of course, having to mention the police phone call and all. No wonder the boy had looked put out. But he hadn't denied his car was at the loch, said he'd run out of petrol. Just the kind of thing he might do.

Who had seen his car, he'd wanted to know. Who said?

Willie was pretty sure he knew the answer to that one. The police themselves would have seen Eric's car. They'd probably been cruising the road on the outlook for drunk drivers, perhaps even Donald himself. They must have heard how bad he'd been lately.

The way things looked, it was a damned pity they hadn't caught him, poor bugger. But of course they would have been called away to yon accident in the Kames.

"So you ran out of petrol," Sergeant Fraser was saying, "and what time would that have been?"

"It wis aboot half past ten. I hed a petrol can ida boot but when I lookit it wis empty. So I walkit inta Brugafirt ta Hamish's."

The hands were clasped tight.

"That's where you were going anyway?"

"Yes. We took Hamish's car."

"And where did you go?"

There was a very slight pause, then Eric said, "We heard dey wir a pairty in Waas, but we couldna fin it. Hamish laekly got it wrong."

"Waas? Quite a distance to go!"

"Yes, it wis a complete waste o time. So we ran Derek hom an sat in aside him an watched a film."

It sounded like the kind of aimless stuff that young folk often ended up doing.

Eric leaned forward and his fair wavy hair fell over his forehead. There was a photo of him a bit like that, taken on a windy day when he was six. Laughing at his dad.

And now, opposite Willie, every fingernail in Eric's clenched brown hands stood out white.

Willie felt suddenly weak and sick at his stomach. He rose to his feet and put peats in the Rayburn. His fingers felt thick and clumsy among the crumbly blue clods, and he bent to sweep the scattered möld.

"So," Sergeant Fraser said, "did Hamish run you back to your car?"

"Yes," said Eric. "Wi *his* can o petrol. His een wis full."

The sergeant laughed.

Willie remembered a red petrol canister in the front of Eric's car. It was right enough! He sat back down in the armchair.

"So what time was that, then, Eric?"

"Weel, I'm no awful sure, laek I said afore, but I tink I cam hom aboot tree o'clock. We sat in Derek's till da late film finished, an dat wis efter two."

"And you didn't see any signs of the camper around then?"

"No, weel, laek I wis sayin, it wis lashin doon wi rain, an I didna hing aroond. I got da petrol in da car, dan she wis still headin up da brae, so I hed ta go up ta da hill-rodd end an turn. Dan I headed for hom as fast as I could. I never saw anything."

The body would have been there, Willie thought. So the folk said. He'd heard it all from Charlie Henderson when he'd phoned about the sheep drench. But it wouldn't have been visible in the car's headlights. It had been down over the banking, so Meg Inkster had told Charlie. And Meg Inkster was a sensible woman. The story would be right. Nobody coming from the Brugafirth direction could possibly have seen the body from a car.

From the other direction though, it would have been possible.

"Where did your friend turn his car?"

Willie found himself holding his breath. But the answer came easily.

"He reversed up ta da hill-rodd end. He laeks ta shaa aff."

Well, that would surely be all now. What a lot of questions he'd asked the boy. Were they all necessary? Suppose Eric had been seeing some lass or other, why on earth should he have to tell a bloody policeman about it? What possible difference could it make where the boy had been? Was he trying to find out if Eric had been drinking too?

Willie hadn't heard Eric coming in. But maybe his mother would have heard the car, if anybody needed to check. She didn't sleep well.

Hamish would vouch for Eric. Derek would too.

Sergeant Fraser got to his feet. He smiled at Eric and Willie. They got up.

"Well, now, that's that. Thank you, Eric. Thank you, Willie. Sorry to have troubled you."

"Dat's aa right, Sergeant," said Willie. "I widna laek your job."

They stood at the outside door a moment. Up on the hill, all Mary's windows were shining in the cold evening sunlight.

"Ah, it's a sad business," said the sergeant. "Just a young chap, and so far from home. Ah well, Willie, I'd better get on." He headed for the police car.

In the kitchen, Eric was lighting a cigarette.

"Weel," said Willie, "yon's yon."

"Yes."

There wasn't much to say.

"Did du ken dee Uncle John wis comin ower da night?"

"Is he?"

"He's comin ta see dee graandmidder."

"Oh, of coorse! Babsy deed!" There was a flash of contact in Eric. "Is Granny aa right? Is she upset?"

"She's aa right, I tink. But du could geng in alang a meenit, maybe."

"I will, efter Meg's gone."

Willie sat down. Eric switched on the TV. It was a game show. Shrieks of laughter and southern accents. There would be no more conversation.

Willie looked at his son and felt sorry for him, as he often did. Young folk ought to be happy.

He said, against the manic sound, "John'll laekly be goin sooth ta da funeral. Der a boat da moarn's night."

"Uh-huh."

Willie rose and turned down the volume. Eric looked up in surprise.

"John'll be goin ta Leith ta Babsy's funeral. I'm no goin. I windered, wid du go in my place?"

Eric looked horrified, then a slow blush came over his face. He looked away, and tapped his cigarette several times on the edge of the peat bucket.

"A funeral is no sae bad," said Willie, "when it's an aald body. Du hardly kent Babsy. An du could see Robert's boys, an hae anidder look at Edinburgh."

He leaned towards Eric, anxiously. "It wid be a brak for dee."

"Some brak," said Eric, with a shaky laugh, "a funeral!"

But he looked at his father with a strange, half-childlike look, and he said, "I'll tink aboot it."

There was the sound of footsteps and a tap on the kitchen door. Meg Inkster's head peeped in.

"Meg?" Willie rose. "Come in."

"Thanks, Willie, but I canna bide. I'm just been in aside dee midder, an poor sowl, she's gettin braaly distressed, does du ken."

Eric switched off the TV.

"I towt at maybe Jessie Anderson wid a come ower tae her for a start. She wid need someen ta be wi her. I could phone an ax Jessie."

Good idea, thought Willie. The very thing.

"Oh yes, yes, dat wid be fine, Meg. Wid du dö dat? Tell her I'll come an fetch her. Oh — use wir phone!"

Meg stepped, neat and competent, to the phone. And there it was, all arranged in a minute. Jessie's loud and kindly sympathy filled the room.

"Poor Cissie! She's bound ta be feelin Babsy's death. Of coorse I'll come ower! I can come right noo!"

Meg put down the phone, frowning.

"Willie," she said, "Cissie is upset, but it's no really because o Babsy. She's turnin da hoose upside doon lookin for a photo o Davie."

Shetland Black

──────────── **Chapter 9** ────────────

Mary

"An what's Dad up tae da night, Mam? Can I spaek tae him?"

Mary Jamieson held the phone very tightly and said evenly, "He's no in eenoo, Joanne. He's doon da rodd at da fish. He'll be vexed he's missed dee."

"Oh weel, better luck next time. An Mam, when yon sister o mine phones, tell her ta gie me a ring. I'm no heard fae her in weeks, an I can never get trow tae her in yon nurses' hom."

"I'll tell her. She'll maybe phone on Sunday."

"I towt she might a come doon ta Falkirk for a day or two. I get a week aff noo in April, an efter aa, it's no dat far."

"Oh dat wid be fine. I'll tell her. So dan, Joanne, I'll ring aff noo."

"Is everything aa right, Mam? Du soonds kinda . . ."

"I'm fine, joy. Just a bit tired. I'm been spring-cleanin."

"As if dy hoose wis needin it! Weel, cheerio dan."

"Cheerio, joy. Gie me love ta Andrew. Guid bliss dee."

There was a photo of the two lasses beside the phone. Chris and Joanne. So bonny they were, and so clever. Both nurses, just what she had wanted them to be. Excellent nurses. And Joanne had married a doctor. Doctor Andrew MacFarlane. Except now he was a surgeon, you weren't really supposed to call him doctor any more. It was back to mister. Surely there should be a title for the job.

Chris's Tuesday letter was still in the drawer. Donald hadn't seen it.

Yes, they were doing fine, the lasses. How Meg would have loved to have daughters like them! Poor Meg. Never able to have bairns, and then her man leaving her like that. Having to fend for herself for so long, wearing herself out running that shop. Sometimes she hardly had time to clean the house.

Surely Meg would have left Cissie's by now! She'd been there nearly an hour. Mary headed for the kitchen window. One thing for sure, Meg would know what to do. She'd be along any minute.

The police car was down at Clivagarth.

From the bedroom upstairs, there came the sound of slow footsteps. Donald had been lying down most of the afternoon, refusing food, eating aspirins, complaining of a headache. In a few moments, he appeared at the kitchen door, unshaven, clothes askew. His face was flushed and his eyes bright, but he looked straight at her.

"Da sergeant'll be comin," he said.

He looked a sight.

"Geng an shave dee, can du no? Comb dee hair."

"No."

"I wiss du wid pit on a better-laek jumper."

"For Christ's sake, wumman!" He fairly glared at her. "Der a man dead! What ta hell does it maitter aboot a jumper, or onything idder?"

Mary picked up a dishcloth, opened the cutlery drawer, and began to polish the spoons. She rubbed very carefully, buffing the silver into shining reflections, spoon by spoon.

Donald sat down by the window. "Weel," he said, "aa you can dö is tell da truth."

Mary polished intently.

"I spak ta da boy. I mind dat ower weel. His name wis Terry. Freendly kind o fellow. Faider hed a garage in Wellington. Couldna say whan he left da pub."

There were three more spoons to shine.

"Du said I cam hame at da back o wan."

Reflections in spoons were strange. Distorted, or upside down.

"I canna mind whan I cam hame. I canna mind comin hame. I'm goin ta tell him dat."

Shine. Shine. Shine.

"He's goin ta say I wis hed ower muckle drink, an I'm goin ta say, dat's right, I did, but it'll be da last time."

A spoon clattered to the floor.

"Da last time?"

He was red-faced, urgent, almost tearful. "When du wis at Cissie's, I phoned yon number at du gae me afore. I'm goin ta Lerook ta yon Alcohol Advice place on Monday. I'll tell da sergeant dat."

27

Mary stood unable to speak.

He leaned forward. "What else can I do, Mary? It's a godless thing. Maybe it wis me at wis da death o yon boy. I maybe hat intae him an killed him. I canna mind wan fuckin thing aboot it!"

He sobbed into his clenched hands.

"No!" she cried. "Don't say dat! Du didna kill him!"

The bowed head shook violently from side to side.

A car engine stopped at the roadside. Sergeant Fraser had arrived.

Donald sat up, suddenly calm.

"We'll get dis by wi," he said.

Shetland Black

──────────────── **Chapter 10** ────────────────

Jack

Jack Thompson carefully polished the Audi, and kept half an eye on Martin, who was careering around the patio in his baby-walker. Some turn of speed with the peerie fellow now, he thought.

Marilyn was loading washing-machine and dishwasher in the back kitchen. She was in one of her untouchable moods. She often came back from Amy's like that.

Amy was a bloody bad influence. Left her man last year, taking his bairns away, demanding and getting a council house of her own. And now she was about to ask for half of Jim's house, and everything else the poor bastard possessed.

She was a bad influence all right. Marilyn had changed. So lively, so bubbly she used to be. Sparkling, right across a room. Heads used to turn when you took her anywhere. Everything was fun.

Martin came dangerously near the scalloped edge of the patio. For the tenth time, Jack rushed to turn him on to a safer circuit.

It had to be tiring looking after his nibs all day. Marilyn was played out a lot of the time. Maybe she could do with a holiday.

It was easy, wasn't it? Just buy her something. A holiday, a weekend away. Let her order more new clothes if she wanted. Cash, that was the key. Money could bring back Marilyn's smile.

The Audi gleamed, beautiful, efficient steel.

If he were to no longer have so much money, would Marilyn smile for him then?

Marilyn appeared at the patio door.

"Gordon's on da phone. He canna win ower, he says. He's gotten some kind o bug." She retrieved Martin, who was unwilling. "Come on noo, it's time for dee bath. Be a good boy."

Jack took the call in the garage.

"Weel, Gordon, what's dis at's happened ta dee?"

"Oh it's some shite at's goin aroond, surely. Hell of an upset gut."

29

"I hear dee. Weel, I hoop it doesna hadd dee lang."

"Sae dö I. I hed da police sergeant alang me afore taytime an I could hardly sit still lang enough ta spaek tae him!"

"Police sergeant? What's du been doin?"

"It wis aboot yon New Zealand boy at wis ida pub da streen. Of coorse, du's been sleepin aa day, is du heard aboot it?"

"Him at wis dead at Litlagill? Yes, I heard it fae Tom at da garage when I wis phonin him earlier on. Weel, did du see da fellow at da pub?"

"Yea, I saw him, but I never spak tae him mesell. He yarned ta Donald for a while."

"Weel, da sergeant need hardly a buddered dee."

"Weel, I wis able ta tell him whan da boy left da pub, for he guid oot da door afore me an Jacqueline, an we were hame at eleeven o'clock ta see da boxing. I dönna ken what cam o him efter dat. Naebody seemed ta be seen him. He wis swayin a bit apon his feet, but he wis managin, an I towt he wis just gyaain ta da böd. God knows what he wis doin at Litlagill."

"Hit's a bad thing if he's been run doon an left lyin."

"Hellish, man! But naebody'll ken da right wye o it till Monday or Tuesday when da post-mortem comes trow, so folk widna need ta spaek aboot it. Da wye at some is gyaain on, dey hae Donald ida clink already."

"Weel, Gordon, dat man is been a bloody danger eence ower aften. Does he hae ta kill someen afore onybody wid report him?"

"Poor sod, I tink ill aboot him. He wid laekly never ken if he hat da boy or no. He'll be hells cut up."

"Huh. So he bloody well should be."

"Jack, he maybe never cam near da boy!"

"Weel, maybe no, but it looks braaly laekly, doesn' it? An I have no sympathy for him. Feckless bloody alcoholic. Just laek my owld man. Finest o sowls in company, self-centred bastard underneath."

"Weel, I'm no gyaain ta argue wi dee. We'll see what happens."

"Yon wis surely been a braaly bad accident ida Kames, Tom wis sayin. Een o dem in Aberdeen in intensive care?"

"Yes, da taxi-driver, I believe. Critical condition. Da idder twa is in Lerook, braaly shakken up. So he's been some night o 'im da streen. An me wi da scoor! Jack — I'll hae ta go! Will du come alang for dee welder, dan?"

"Na, heth, I'm gyaain on shift shortly an I'm in nae hurry for him. I ken whaar he is, keep du him. I hoop du's shön better."

Shetland Black

Chapter 11

Meg, Saturday Evening

Meg opened the door of Mary's side porch and quietly set three pints of milk just inside. The sergeant was still in the house, and she didn't want to intrude. She could, of course, have waited till he'd gone, but she was reluctant.

How on earth would Mary be feeling? Meg really ought to see her. She'd need somebody to speak to. Probably more than Cissie had. Meg was maybe the only person Mary might talk to.

But it was nearly eight o'clock, and Meg had a problem of her own.

Not that Evan Ritchie was really a problem. He was still a diversion, a welcome newcomer to her demanding life. Not demanding much himself — not yet. Soon, if he stuck around, he might start demanding. Then she would have to think. But for the moment, everything was relaxed, and she longed more than anything else for that relaxation, for the fact of his not requiring anything of her, for the escape of talking, or not talking, about the whole bloody awful long suffocating day.

God forgive me, she thought, I can't face Mary, not just yet. She quickly walked the fifty yards home.

He answered the phone at the second ring.

"Meg? I was just coming over. What is it?"

She took a deep breath. "Wid you mind if I cam ower ta you instead?"

"Of course not. Are you OK?"

"Yes. It's just — I tink I'd laek ta get oot o here for a while." Her voice was shaking. For goodness sake.

"I'll come and fetch you."

"No, I'll tak da car!"

"You know best!" Pause. "Will you stay over?"

Warmth, strength and refuge. And it was a straight question, not a demand.

"Yes, I maybe will."

"What will my neighbours say?" She could hear Evan smiling. Could picture him smiling, the tanned face creasing up.

"It'll be dark. Dey'll no see."

"I wouldn't bet on it. My reputation will be in tatters."

"I doot dat happened a while ago!"

"Now, Meg, what did you tell me about not listening to gossip?"

He was teasing. He sounded bloody pleased with himself, on the other end of the line. Meg stood alone in her cold house, listening to him sounding pleased with himself twelve miles away.

"It wis me at fan yon boy dead dis moarnin. Do you have any idea what it's been laek da day?"

There was silence, then Evan said, "Meg, I'm sorry. I hadn't heard that. For Christ's sake, don't cry. Sit down, I'm coming to fetch you."

Meg put down the phone, wiped her eyes, sat down and took a deep breath. She reflected ruefully that perhaps she had been the one to start making demands.

Shetland Black

──────────────── **Chapter 12** ────────────────

Jessie

B y ten o'clock, Jessie Anderson was beginning to lose confidence. She liked to think of herself as a capable body, a source of good sense, someone who could be relied upon to sort things out. Only an hour ago, she had been certain that she would soon be able to reassure poor Cissie that there was no possibility of the boy at Litlagill being any relation of hers.

She had made Cissie tea, then poured her a large glass of whisky with lemonade. Cissie rarely drank, but perhaps it might relax her. Jessie had never seen her friend so tense and distressed. Jessie had taken to the phone, sure of finding someone with information about the New Zealander's family background. After all, the boy had been in Brugafirth since Thursday night.

It had been disappointing to find Nessie Clark, the böd caretaker, so unhelpful. She had been going out to the playgroup sale of work when the boy arrived on Thursday evening, and hadn't had a great deal of time for conversation. She'd hardly seen him since. Though of course she had been able to identify him, as far as she could. Fair hair, slim, pleasant-looking boy. What a terrible thing to happen. Nessie would not be able to get it all out of her mind for a good while. What a shock it had been, police at the door first thing in the morning, still, that was nothing to the shock for his poor folk in Wellington. No, no, he hadn't said anything about relations. Well, my mercy, of course, it would be too much of a coincidence for him to be a relation of Cissie Hendry's.

Meg Inkster's phone rang without reply. Jessie called the Friday shop assistants. Only Annie Brown was at home. She had actually served the New Zealand boy but he hadn't said anything about looking for relations or anything. Why?

The local registrar lived in Houbister. Jessie tried his number. No, the New Zealander hadn't come to look at his records. Mind, somebody had phoned on Friday morning but had rung off before he'd had time to answer. Good heavens, was that the story?

Jessie mentally reviewed the people who were reputed to have been at the pub on Friday. She couldn't phone Bob Tulloch himself; he'd be busy behind the bar right now. Folk said he was pretty uneasy about the whole affair, what with the state Donald was supposed to be in. Bob Tulloch might get into trouble for allowing it.

Anyway, Bob was not renowned for making conversation with his customers. Kathy Bruce, now, she worked in the pub sometimes . . . but not on Fridays, apparently.

Jessie resorted to Gordon Morrison's wife, Jacqueline, a sensible lass who might give her some sources. Well yes, they had seen the boy, he'd left the pub at the same time as they had, about eleven. She'd noticed him speaking briefly to Alastair and Maurice, but most of the time he seemed to be sitting with Donald. And wasn't it terrible? And how was Cissie, hadn't her sister died, poor soul? What?

Cissie sat on the settee, clasping a snapshot, eyes burning Jessie. Twice she said, "Eric's left his jacket. He guid oot in such a hurry." Several times she said, "Meg saw his face. Get Meg ta come doon."

Willie Hendry came in out of the blustery night, followed by his brother John. Jessie was relieved to see John. Holding a conversation with Willie was like pulling teeth. They sat down, Jessie rose to make tea, and Cissie let her. The brothers exchanged looks.

Cissie was glad to see her sons, but seemed little concerned with talk of funerals, flowers and announcements in the paper. John said matter-of-factly that he would see to all that.

"Sam verse as du hed for Robbie, will dat dö?"

"Yes, yes, onything you laek."

"Eric is tinkin he'll come ta Leith wi me."

"He said dat, yes. Poor ting Eric." She looked down at the photo in her hand. "I shaaed him Davie's photo." She handed it to Willie, eagerly. "It's no a bad photo, is it, after aa?"

Jessie, handing out cups, thought Willie looked as puzzled as she was. It was not a good photo, not by any stretch of the imagination. She had expected it to be a proper old studio portrait, formal and crisp in a fading cardboard frame. It was a yellowing amateur snap of a laughing young man with fair hair and a slim build. Not close enough or well enough focused for Jessie, who could not remember ever having seen Davie Pearson.

Cissie said, "It's just foo I mind him. Aye laachin. Poor Davie." Her eyes filled with tears. Jessie moved to her side.

Cissie looked at the three of them. "We could surely get da boy's hame address fae da police, dö you tink? Dey wid surely gie it tae wis, if dey kent da circumstances?"

Willie Hendry looked helplessly at Jessie, who tried to rise to the occasion. "Weel I wid tink," she said, as authoritatively as possible, "at da police wid maybe be able ta mak enquiries on your behalf."

"Dey maybe could," said Cissie. "Wid du phone an ax da sergeant?"

"Mam," said John, "it's Setterday night. We canna phone him eenoo. An du kens, it's really no awful laekly at dis boy hed onything ta dö wi Davie at all."

"Maybe no. But maybe he did. Meg said he wis kinda laek Eric. Why did he come here, at dis time o year? On his ain?"

Willie said abruptly, "I tink he wis laekly bird-watchin. He wis in da rodd aboot denner-time. He guid walkin oot aroond da Ness."

"Did du see him?"

"Weel — I saw him fae a piece aff, getting oot o Jack Thompson's car. Dan he guid awa oot ower an I never saw him ageen."

"Der's anidder een we could phone, Jessie. Jack Thompson!"

It was soon done, with no success.

"He's on night shift, Cissie. I got yon snippit wife o his. Never even axed if she could tak a message."

"We'll phone him da moarn."

It had definitely been a mistake to give Cissie the whisky. Her face was red and her eyes were too bright.

"Try Meg again," she said.

"Cissie," said Jessie patiently, "Meg most be oot. I'm tried her tree times."

"She's maybe in aside Mary," John suggested.

Cissie heaved a sigh and nodded. There was a silence.

Jessie told the brothers about her enquiries so far. "An Jacqueline says at da boy wis spaekin ta Alastair an Maurice for a start. Weel, I ken I needna try ony o dem apon a Setterday night. An apparently da een at he spak tae da maist wis Donald. Noo, I dönna tink we should budder him da night, should we?"

"Donald?" Cissie was contemptuous, "What wid *he* mind?"

Willie said, "I dönna tink we should tell him aboot dis at all — eenoo."

"Or Mary edder," said John. "Dey hae enough ta tink aboot."

"Is du been alang dem da night, John?" Jessie enquired.

"No yet. I'll hae ta look alang as I geng hame. I hardly ken what ta say. I'll no say onything aboot dis, though."

"Dey'll surely no hear it fae ony idder wye," said Jessie, uncomfortably.

They sat silent. Cissie seemed deep in her own thoughts. A growing number of local people would soon know about her crazy notion. Jessie told herself she had only been trying to help. Her intentions had been good. What else could she have done?

She wished that one of the brothers would reassure her a little. But John seemed preoccupied, and Willie was as dour as ever.

Shetland Black

—————————————— **Chapter 13** ——————————————

Midnight

Willie slept uncomfortably on his mother's settee. Jessie had promised to come back again next day, but he and John had agreed that Cissie should not be left on her own tonight. The woman was ill.

Upstairs, Cissie tossed and turned.

Eric was on his way home, driving more slowly than usual. Hadn't felt like staying at the stupid party. Folk kept asking too many bloody questions. Hamish was being so damned awkward. Couldn't relax at all.

Donald was still sitting in the armchair where the sergeant had left him almost four hours earlier. On the coffee table in front of him was a bottle of rum, three-quarters empty.

In the kitchen, Mary watched the hands of the clock reach midnight. When they did, she rose and opened the side door for the twentieth time, looking for a light in Meg's house. There was none. Meg had been out for hours. At half past eight her door had been locked. She wasn't there. The whole world was darkness. Mary walked back into the kitchen, took two tablets, went upstairs to Joanne's little front bedroom and closed the door.

In Roselea, Marilyn lay in bed looking at an old black and white movie, unable to sleep. The bedroom door was open in case Martin cried.

Miles away, Meg slept, and did not dream.

Shetland Black

———————————— **Chapter 14** ————————————

Jack, Sunday Morning

Jack lifted his smiling son for a good-morning cuddle, then lowered him carefully into his playpen and surrounded him with bright, safe toys.

"Now dan, sit dere an play dee for a peerie while, please."

Marilyn was already in the bedroom, and slipped into bed as he came in. He would have liked her to wait, and let him take off her dressing-gown, but he wouldn't complain. New-washed and shining from the shower, she looked and smelt lovely. Felt lovely. He took her fiercely in his arms.

She stroked him, she smiled at him, she moved as he wished, she was not unwilling, but by and by he knew she had no heart for him this morning. He was disappointed.

Afterwards he looked at her, lying there unmoved and unreachable.

"Can du never relax when Martin is up? Is du aye listenin for him?"

She turned her head away. "I'm sorry, Jack. I canna help it."

There was a peerie wail from the sitting-room, and she was springing up, reaching for her dressing-gown. In the pocket was a tissue; she blew her nose. There was a tear on her cheek.

"Marilyn!" he reached out for her. "Lat him wait!"

The phone rang, shrill and sudden, at the bedside. Jack swore, and picked it up. Marilyn disappeared.

The voice on the line was urgent. "Hello? Hello? Is dat Jack Thompson?"

"Spaekin."

"Hello, I'm sorry ta budder you but it's very important. Did you gie da New Zealand boy a lift in your car yesterday?"

"Yesterday?"

"No, no, of coorse, it wid a been Friday. Friday aboot denner-time. Willie said you slippit him aff an he guid walkin oot aroond da Ness."

"Wha am I spaekin tae? Whit is dis?"

"Oh, I'm sorry. It's Cissie Hendry, Cissie fae Clivagarth. Cissie Pearson at used ta be."

Cissie Hendry! Willie's mother. Jack had hardly spoken two words to her. The poor body was distressed. Maybe she was doitin. Christ, what next?

"So it's Cissie. Right Cissie, now at denner-time on Friday I wis sleepin in me bed because I'm on nights eenoo. So I doot Willie is got it wrang. Is dis da boy at Litlagill you're spaekin aboot? I never laid eyes on him, poor craiter."

"I'm tryin ta fin someen at's spokken tae him, because he might be Davie's graandson. I need ta ken wha he is."

Well, there was no point in asking questions. "I'm sorry, Cissie, I canna help you. It wisna me at gae him da lift."

"Oh I'm sorry. I'm awful sorry ta be buddered you for naethin. Willie towt it wis your car, you see."

From the sitting-room, Marilyn cried, "Martin, *no!*"

Jack stared down at the empty bed. Then he said, "Weel of coorse, it might a been Marilyn."

"Could you ax her?" Cissie's voice was shrill.

"I'll ax her."

"An will you lat me ken?"

"Yes, yes, we'll lat you ken. So cheerio dan."

"Oh thank you. Davie wis me . . ."

Jack heard no more. He pulled on his jeans and stood up.

He could hear Marilyn moving round the kitchen. The kettle was boiling. The sun was shining. It was a bright, breezy day outside. And his night shifts were finished. He'd intended to do without sleep today, to spend the day with Marilyn and Martin. He still could.

Marilyn didn't tell lies. She told the truth even when it hurt. She'd always been like that.

There was a queasiness in his stomach as he walked into the kitchen.

"Wha wis yon?" she asked, busy at the sink.

"Cissie Hendry."

"Cissie Hendry! What wis she wantin?"

"She seemed ta be in a distress ta fin oot aboot da New Zealand boy. Tinks he might be someen's graandson."

Marilyn stopped working. "Why wis she phonin dee?"

The words came out in a rush. "Willie towt I gae da boy a lift in da rodd, but of coorse I didna. Did du?"

Her shoulders seemed to give a little and she said nothing for a moment. Then she said, "Yes, I did. He wis hitchin twartree mile oot a Brugafirt as I cam fae Lerook. He wanted ta see kittiwakes. I ran him as far as Donald's salmon pier."

Jack felt as if he might be sick.

"Marilyn. We spak aboot dis boy yesterday. Du never mentioned at du wis ever seen him. Why no?"

Why wouldn't she bloody well face him? He grabbed her shoulder and pulled her around. She lifted her face defiantly.

"Do I have ta tell dee everything I do?"

She sounded like Amy, brass-necked Amy. Standing there in her expensive dressing-gown, in her fancy kitchen.

The boy had left the pub at eleven. And nobody knew where he had gone. Maybe everybody knew. Nobody would tell *him*.

"He wis here, wisn' he, at night? Dat's why he wis in dis rodd! He cam here ta see dee!"

She shook her head vehemently. "No! He did not!"

It was a lie, a damned lie. She was lying to him.

"Bitch!"

Fear and fury came out of his mouth, foul and terrible. He watched her shudder and shrink from him, try to speak, then turn and run. He followed her as far as the locked bathroom door, refusing to hear her sobs on the other side. Only when Martin began to howl behind him did he realise he was still shouting.

He bent down to the peerie frightened face, but could not help. He called through the bathroom door.

"Du better look ta Martin. I'm goin."

He leapt into the Audi and headed out the road with no clear idea of where he was going. On the other side of Brugafirth, he stopped at a lay-by, and waited for his hands to stop shaking.

He could only remember that she had denied everything, and that he hadn't hit her. But the words, the words had been violence enough.

Shetland Black

———————————— **Chapter 15** ————————————

Meg, Sunday Morning

Meg and Evan ate bacon rolls for breakfast. The sun shone in Evan's kitchen window.

"I wish I had a view like you have," he said.

They looked at the cluster of houses and the sloping park full of sheep.

"I hardly ever look at my view. I wiss I hed central heating laek you have."

Evan grinned. "Nobody's ever contented, are they?"

He sat opposite, comfortable in an old soft shirt. Meg remembered how she had clung to him last night, and was grateful. Now she sat demurely sipping tea, and was equally grateful for that distancing. It was nearly ten o'clock. Soon she would have to go home.

Evan reached into a cupboard. "Fixed your hair-drier. Wasn't much wrong with it."

"Oh, splendid!" She smiled. "You're savin me a fortune. I'd need to pay you."

"No problem," he said. "I'll add it to the bill at the end of the month. Prompt payment expected on the sixth. No cheques, please."

Meg felt she was giggling like a schoolgirl, then she realised something.

"I towt you were goin sooth next time you cam ashore."

"Well, I am, but not the first week." He looked a little displeased. "The baby's being christened. I'd best avoid that carry-on. But I'm not going to miss Lisa's birthday, whatever Liz might say. So I'll go down the second week."

Meg nodded, and felt awkward.

Evan's children, smiling on the wall, looked like him. Lisa, especially, had the brown eyes and dark hair. Robert, a little taller, had the leanness, but lighter colouring. Perhaps he was more like Liz. There were no photographs of Liz.

"What do you buy for a girl of fifteen, Meg? Any ideas?"

That needed discussion. It was well past ten before she found a moment to say, "Evan, I think I would need ta go."

He looked down at her and lifted an eyebrow. "Stayed too long, have you, Meg?"

She blushed. He laughed. "It's OK! I know you have to see Mary. You told me often enough last night."

"I'm sorry. I'm just feelin guilty aboot no seein her da streen. She's been awful tensed up aa week. Donald is pretty bad eenoo, an it's tellin apon her. No at she ever *says* very muckle, but . . . I'm fairt ta tink what she might be laek *noo*."

"You," said Evan, touching the tip of her nose, "had had enough last night. You can't carry all of it, Meg. Everybody needs a break."

His ex-wife thought he was an absolute bastard. He had assured Meg that she was right, he had been no good as a husband. He had understood it meant earning money, and he had earned more money in the construction of Sullom Voe Oil Terminal than he had ever thought possible. He had been allowed home one week in every six, had spent much of it keeping up with old pals, had hardly ever seen his infant children, and had spent what seemed like a fortune on the horses. When he went to work offshore, he was home more often but behaved no better. All this he freely admitted. It had taken him a long time, he said, to grow up.

The dark eyes looked at Meg.

"I'll have ta go," she said.

In the car, they again discussed the New Zealand boy.

"Do you have any idea why he was there, on that road?"

"Mm — weel, maybe he just mistook da rodd in da dark. Got lost."

"It's right in the opposite direction, come on."

Perhaps she could talk freely. "Well, I did hear wan person sayin at dey saw Marilyn Thompson wi dis boy in her car on Friday. She wis laekly geen him a lift. I did winder if maybe he took it intae his head ta visit her. Please don't repeat dat."

He gave her a sideways glance. "I won't. But why shouldn't he visit her?"

"Weel — I suppose, nae raeson why. It's just at her man is wirkin nights just noo."

Flicker of eyebrows. "Marilyn Thompson. Would that be Jack Thompson's wife? Blonde?"

"Dat's her."

"Mm. She wouldn't have invited him, would she?"

Meg felt defensive of a fellow female. "What maks you say dat?"

"Looks like Liz."

No reply to that.

Houses straggled into peat moor, into open hill. The road was quiet. One Ford van.

By and by, Evan said, "It's weird, this idea of Cissie's. There couldn't be anything in it, could there?"

"Oh, I widna tink so. Somebody wid ken if he hed local connections. He wis sure ta tell folk aboot dem, an be axin aroond. An nobody's ever said a wird. It canna be possible. Dey most be thousands o Pearsons in New Zealand."

They were through Brugafirth. Evan slowed down for the Whalvoe junction. He waved a hand towards the opposite side of the road.

"Now *that's* where we were on Friday night, right *there*, when that taxi turned out in front of us. Angus had to brake so hard, the rest of us slid all over the mini-bus. Wet roads, too. Stupid bugger."

"An you said dat wis aboot twal o'clock?"

"Might have been half past. Think we left Hillswick about quarter past."

"I still canna tink what dat taxi wid a been doin in Whalvoe. Aless it wis ony pals o Eric's or something."

"Maybe someone had visitors."

They passed the loch and came to the passing-place, where Meg hadn't wanted to stop the previous night. This time they got out and looked.

Birds called, unseen, all round. Two sheep, heavy with lamb, ambled out of their way. High overhead, a jet plane left snow-feather trails in the breezy blue sky.

"Dat's whaar he wis." Meg stood close. The air was chill.

There were a lot of stones.

Evan looked at the slope of the banking and the turn of the road.

"I suppose," he said, "I ought to tell the police about the taxi. If it comes to that."

"If it comes ta dat."

It was eleven o'clock as they turned the last corner. The first thing they saw was a white estate car at Clivagarth.

"My God, Evan, it's da doctor!"

He reached out a hand.

"Go ta Mary's, Evan, please! She'll surely ken what's happened."

Donald was asleep in an armchair in the sitting-room, an empty bottle and an empty half-bottle lying in front of him. On the unit by his side was propped a note in Mary's handwriting: *At Clivagarth. Mam ill.*

It took two minutes to get back to her own house and phone Cissie's. Eric answered, sounding very young and uncertain.

"Evan, Cissie is hed a stroke. An oor ago. She's aye hed high blood pressure."

They looked at each other. Evan said, "I suppose you'll need to go down. I'll better go."

They stood a moment. Then she rose on her toes and kissed him before he left. Wondered if it was the right thing to do.

The doctor's car was leaving Clivagarth. Meg set off for Cissie's.

Shetland Black

————————————— **Chapter 16** —————————————

Willie, Sunday Morning

Willie needed to get outside. The flowered wallpaper was overcoming him, the heating suffocating. His mother lay with closed eyes on her sitting-room bed-settee. He and Eric had done their best to put bedclothes on it, but they hadn't found the right sheets. Nothing seemed to fit.

Eric had fetched Cissie's pillows and duvet from upstairs. Eric had hunted for hot-water bottles, turned up the radiator, brought a water-jug with ice-cubes. Eric had phoned his sister Gail. All off his own bat.

The boy looked terrible. No wonder. Finding Cissie on the floor like that. He'd done well, though. Phoned the doctor, made Cissie comfortable on the floor, covered her with a blanket, run to the barn to shout to Willie, then gone right back again to her side.

Willie must remember to tell Eric that he'd done well. Thelma always said he never praised him enough.

"Du's quick enough ta tell him when he does something wrang!"

Thelma would have been pleased with Eric today.

John would be coming as soon as he could, and bringing Mina. Mary had taken her time coming down. And now she was here, she seemed content just to sit by her mother's side. She'd hardly said a word, not even to the doctor. Just stared. She was under a lot of strain, of course. Cissie taking a stroke was the last thing she needed. The last thing any of them needed.

Could he go now? The doctor had said there was nothing they could do but wait. He'd be back later. The first seventy-two hours were critical. Cissie needed absolute quiet and rest.

It was far too bloody hot in here. There was nothing to do. There was no point in all three of them sitting.

Willie rose and turned down the radiator. "I tink I'll hae ta geng an slip oot da dogs. I'll be back in a start."

Eric said, "Der someen comin in."

Willie's heart sank. He would have to stay a while yet.

Footsteps hesitated in the kitchen, then a knock came at the ben door. It was Meg Inkster. A breath of cool air came in with her.

"I saw da doctor laevin." Meg looked down at the fiercely sleeping face. "Foo is she?"

Willie wondered how many times he would have to repeat the story, how many faces would soften as Meg's just had, how many people would phone. The whole compassion circus was creaking into gear again. All that prying and sympathising. Out there, about to roll in the road towards him.

But Meg was nodding and saying to Eric that he had done all the right things and how lucky it was he had been there. Eric blushed and shifted his feet. Meg was looking at Mary.

"I'm awful sorry, Mary, at I never wan alang you da streen. I hed ta go awey."

Mary barely inclined her head. Meg looked searchingly at her, then at Willie.

And then she was saying how she was sure Willie had work he was needing to do, and maybe Eric as well, and how she could sit with Mary for a while till some of the others arrived. And Willie found himself in the kitchen, with the door closing behind him, and the sun shining outside.

But Meg stood at his side. She spoke quietly.

"Foo wis Cissie da streen efter I left you? Wis she still on aboot Davie an da photo?"

Willie started. He had forgotten all about that.

"Oh heevens, yes. She fan da photo aa right, no at he wis awful clear or onything. An she got dat wund up at Jessie phoned aroond tryin ta fin someen at wis spoken ta da boy, ta see if he said onything aboot his faimily."

"Did she ax Donald?"

"Na, we pat her aff o dat."

"You were right. It's ill enough for dem eenoo. What does du tink o Mary da day?"

What was he supposed to say to that? "Weel, she's hardly said a wird fae she cam."

"She's fillt hersell wi Valium, or something braaly laek it, dat's why."

48

"Good God." Willie stared.

"I tink, " said Meg, "she's been takin dem for a while, back an fore."

Their silence was broken by Eric, slipping out of the sitting-room.

"Is du needin a haand, Dad?"

Willie had expected him to say he was off somewhere in the car.

"Weel, fine dat. We'll maybe get da sooth trow sheep fed afore denner-time. Better pit on some idder claes."

Meg said she would make some tea and sandwiches for about one o'clock. She seemed to have come prepared; a plastic carrier bag lay on the table.

"I'll better go in ta Mary. Oh, but how did Jessie come on wi her phonin aroond? Did she fin oot onything aboot da boy?"

"Na. Naebody kent onything. Mam wis anxious ta spaek ta Jack Thompson, but he wisna in."

"Jack Thompson?" Eric sounded surprised.

"He gae da boy a lift in da rodd on Friday. I saw da car."

Meg frowned. "Na, Willie, I tink it wis Marilyn at hed da car on Friday. Somebody idder saw dem. Jack is on nights eenoo."

"Marilyn? Oh, it could a been for me. I couldna mak oot wha it wis. I kent it wis der Audi."

Bonnie young lass with a man working nights. Something made sense at last. Meg Inkster was saying nothing. Maybe she thought so too.

"It's a peety dee midder never got ta spaek ta Marilyn. She might a been able ta pit her mind at rest."

Eric moved abruptly to the door, and was gone. The porch door slammed. They looked after him.

"Poor ting," said Meg, and moved towards ben.

Willie stepped out into the sea-bright day, leaving the claustrophobic house to the women.

Shetland Black

——————————————— **Chapter 17** ———————————————

Sunday Afternoon

Cissie lay small and frail under her quilt, eyes closed. Sometimes she seemed restless, moaning occasionally, sometimes muttering scrambled words impossible to understand. It was less frightening for the others when she lay still.

Mary sat in an armchair, quietly watching her mother, or staring out the window at the sea. She would stay here till the doctor came back, at least. Donald would sleep all day. Mary drank the tea handed to her. She greeted newcomers, but it was not a suitable time for speaking to folk. It was so much effort. Folk said such silly things. And as for Meg, she needn't be so concerned now. She hadn't been around when Mary needed her last night.

Mina, John's wife, sat by the window, talking quietly to Gail about everything in general and nothing much in particular. Well, somebody had to make conversation. John had set off after half an hour to help Willie feeding sheep somewhere. Eric and Gail's boyfriend had surely gone too. It would be a long day, and goodness only knew if the old wife would come through it. Cissie was a game lady, but everything had just been too much for her this weekend. Mina wondered uneasily what would happen if Cissie survived but was too weak to look after herself. Mary's household was no place for her, and Willie could never manage. Thelma was such a miss . . . Well, it looked very much like peerie Gail was pregnant. That would at least be something cheerful to look forward to. Not married, of course, but they might get around to it yet . . .

Gail listened to her aunt's endless chatter and hoped she was nodding in the right places. She was sure Cissie was dying. Clivagarth was dying, right before her eyes. There would be nobody at all with a warm hug to meet you, and time for stories and confidences. It had been bearable to come here for Granny's sake. Soon, it would be unbearable, no warmth, no life left at all. Eric was so distant now, and soon he'd be away. And nobody could reach Dad. Gail swallowed hard. The only thing to do was go on, make your own home, your own family, be Mam.

Try to be Mam.

"Excuse me," she said, and went to cry in the bathroom.

Eric and Stewart, Gail's boyfriend, fed Donald's salmon. John had suggested it. Stewart was used to the job, and Eric had often helped before. Taking the boat, the feed bags, lifting, loading, emptying — it was good solid work, a man's job. It was concrete and straightforward; the effort kept you from thinking. Out at the cages, it was a cold peerie world apart.

Meg had got a good fire going in her Rayburn as soon as she came home at two o'clock. By four, the house was warming up, there was a second load of washing in the machine, and she was trying to settle to some ironing. She switched on her kitchen radio, but never managed to listen.

In the park below Roselea, Willie and John heaved bales of hay out of the pick-up. They didn't speak. Alerted sheep came mehh-ing right from the sea banks. Willie eyed them critically as they crowded round. They were in pretty good condition considering the wet winter it had been. They ought to be; he spent enough on them. He knew what to buy, knew exactly what to do. It was a comforting, comfortable feeling. He looked forward to the lambing.

They turned eventually back up towards the road. A peerie dark green Fiesta pulled out from Roselea and headed out the road. There was a flash of blonde hair in the passenger side window.

The brothers looked in on Donald on their way home. Looked into several rooms, and then the bedroom. Donald was in bed, snoring heavily. Trousers and shoes lay jettisoned on the floor. The house smelt of rum.

As they returned to the pick-up, the phone in the house began to ring, but it was too far away to answer.

Shetland Black

────────────── **Chapter 18** ──────────────

Meg, Sunday Evening

Evan rang Meg at five.

"Da doctor's comin back efter taytime. It's been a heavy stroke, though. I don't know if she'll come oot o it."

"Are you going down again?"

"No, no da night, aless dey want me for onything. I'll just phone efter da doctor is been. Da faimily's aa dere noo."

"Donald too?"

"Weel, aless for Donald."

"And how's Mary?"

"She's sittin dere lookin laek a ghost. Dopit ta da eyeballs wi Valium or something. She widna hardly spaek ta me at all."

"Well, it'll be the only way she can cope."

"I ken, but it's horrible ta see."

"Would it be better if she was breaking down and howling?"

"Weel, I suppose no." The kettle on the Rayburn began to sing. "Wid you laek ta come ower da night?"

Hesitation.

"It's aa right, Evan, you dönna have to come. It's no very cheery aroond here eenoo. Never mind. Anidder time."

"Well," he said, "I just had a call from Angus. He was trying to organise a darts team meeting. Typical last-minute stuff. He could have done it on Friday night. I told him I could probably make it. I thought you might be otherwise engaged."

"Yes, yes, of coorse. I ken. Dat's OK. It'll no maitter. Never mind."

Pause.

"Meg, will I come or not? And don't say 'come if you want'!"

Evan wasn't smiling. Meg took a breath.

"Come if you can. Even — even efter da meeting."

"Right," he said, more relaxed. "I'll try to do that. I don't suppose I'll make it before ten."

"Fine."

"Meg, know what Angus was telling me? When he went back down the Kames on Friday night, he came by that accident. Police and ambulance and all were there, he had to wait. And it was the same taxi. The one that nearly hit us. He recognised the number."

"Good Lord. An da taxi-driver is in Aberdeen, isn' he? Unconscious?"

"So they say."

"Da taxi firm wid ken whaar he wis been, though."

"One-man band, Angus says."

"But he wid hae records o some kind, surely."

"I hope so," said Evan. "Anyway, Meg, see you later."

The kind eyes of Cissie Hendry haunted Meg as she prepared and ate her solitary evening meal. Kind, and then so distressed. Eyes rolling under closed lids this morning, as if in a bad dream. Was Cissie dreaming?

Nobody at Clivagarth had tried to phone Marilyn Thompson again. John had phoned his cousin Robert in Leith — obviously they couldn't go to Babsy's funeral now. And then he had phoned Jessie Anderson, and a few more relations. But nobody had suggested phoning Marilyn, or investigating the camper any further.

Perhaps they should. Perhaps if a definite answer could be found, they could get it through to Cissie yet. She might rally a little . . . It might make a difference, might relieve her mind, if you were able to say with certainty, "He's no Davie's graandson, Cissie."

Meg lifted the phone and rang Roselea.

It was a long time before anyone answered. Then a woman's voice, hesitant.

"614342."

It was Jacqueline Morrison. Gordon and she must be visiting.

"Hello. Dis is Meg Inkster here, Jacqueline. Can I spaek ta Marilyn?"

"I'm sorry, Meg, no, du canna. She's no here."

"Oh. Weel, whan will she be back, does du ken? It's kinda important."

There was the definite sound of a door closing, and then Jacqueline said "I dönna ken whan she'll be back, Meg. Dey hed a terrible row dis moarnin an Jack left da hoose. An when he cam back she wis gone. He phoned for Gordon ta come ower."

Misery everywhere. "Dat's terrible. What aboot peerie Martin?"

"She's taen him wi her. Jack tinks she'll be gone ta Amy Hunter in Scallowa."

Meg stared at her empty plate and cold dregs of tea.

"Does du tink dey'll no mak it up?"

"I dönna ken. We're hoopin at he'll phone an spaek tae her."

"I see."

"Meg, foo is Cissie? We heard she wis hed a stroke."

"She's naething great."

"Did dey ever manage ta fin oot onything aboot da New Zealand boy?"

"No." Meg hesitated. "Dat's why I wis phonin Marilyn. I tink she gae him a lift. I wid just a laekit tae a been able ta pit Cissie's mind at rest. But it canna be helpit noo."

"Did du ken at she phoned here hersell dis moarnin?"

"Cissie? Whan?"

"Aboot half past nine. But she didna get Marilyn. She got Jack. An of coorse, it wis da first he kent aboot ony lift . . ."

"Oh God . . ."

"Just dat." Pause. "Jack did say she seemed fairly wrought up."

"She took da stroke aboot ten." Meg pictured Cissie excited, anxious, clutching the phone. "Poor sowl!"

"Does du ken what I wiss?" said Jacqueline. "God forgive me, but I wiss yon bloody boy wid never a left New Zealand."

Shetland Black

Chapter 19

Eric, Sunday Evening

Eric locked up the dogs, walked around to the lee side of the barn and lit a cigarette. He wouldn't go back to the house till the doctor had gone.

It was cold out here, but the lowering sun still shone, and the waves broke silkily over the shingly beach below. On the other side of the water, the banks opened out to the sea, and layers of cletts and headlands lay mysteriously grey in the westerly light. To his left, the isles sheltered Donald's salmon; to the right lay the steep-sided voe and winding valley of Whalvoe.

It was a bonny place, right enough, on a fine night.

It was silly how people got attached to places. Places were just land and sea and rocks. Just geography. The hills and the sea were cold and eternal. They went on for ever. It didn't matter to them whether people were there or not.

People were temporary. People died.

Lots of them died without ever having lived very much. Never been anywhere much, never done anything much. They just died, whether they were good, bad or indifferent.

Granny said you would only die when your time came. At least she'd had a fair amount of time. Mam hadn't.

Neither had Terry Pearson, who had travelled halfway round the world when his time came.

But there was no rule that said life had to be fair.

Eric didn't want to think about Terry Pearson.

The doctor had left at last. He'd go in now, and look at their faces. Look at Gail. He'd know if he looked at Gail.

Gail lived too far away now. And she had Stewart. She'd left Eric to Clivagarth, and Dad. Just left him to it. It was a bloody lonely place, apart from Granny.

Granny.

Eric went in.

In the kitchen, John was on the phone. "Weel, Meg, tanks ta dee for tryin onywye. Yes, yes, we will. So cheerio noo."

Mina was drying dishes, his father standing by the window. Gail and Stewart and Mary must be with Cissie.

"What's da news?"

John said, "She's braaly waek, Eric. Der still a chance, but — no a big een."

"But der still a chance?"

Willie looked up. "She's been kinda waaken. She kent wis."

"She kent you? Dat's a bit better, surely? Wid she ken me?"

His father's face was gentle, as if Eric was about six.

"She maybe wid, Eric. But dönna tink apon it if she doesna."

Mina was asking John what Meg had been saying. John looked hurriedly towards the closed ben door.

"She wis been tryin ta ax Marilyn aboot da New Zealand boy, but Marilyn's no hame. I tink Meg wid a laekit tae a pitten Mam's mind at rest, but it's laekly ower late noo."

Mina sighed and shook her head. They were all silent.

Granny had been really upset last night. And the photo she'd found — it was sixty-odd years old. And yet you'd have thought the man had disappeared yesterday. How she'd gone on about him. He must have been at the back of her mind all the time, the missing brother, the one who went halfway round the world and never came home. Maybe his time came.

She'd always wanted to know what happened to Davie.

Eric went ben, past the silent Mary, and looked at Gail. She'd been crying, but was composed now. Stewart was holding her hand.

"Did she ken dee?" Eric asked.

"I'm no sure. She smiled."

Cissie's eyes were shut. Gold light fell over her bed. Eric sat beside her, back to the window. She would know him. She might not have known Gail, but she would know him.

"Granny?"

Nobody was talking in the kitchen.

"Granny? Granny, is du goin ta spaek ta me?"

The breathing was steady.

"Granny, it's Eric. Waaken up." He grabbed her hand.

Willie stood at her side. "Lat her be, Eric!"

"Granny!" His voice sounded loud and strange in his own ears. "Open dee eyes!"

There was a flicker in the face, a movement of the grey head. Cissie's eyes opened, blinked and slowly focused on the face above her. Eric's hair fell over his forehead.

Cissie looked at Eric, squeezed his hand and began to smile. The smile filled her whole face, warmed the whole room.

"Davie!" she said. "*Davie!*"

She didn't know him. He couldn't see her for tears. But he knew he had to keep holding her hand.

He was aware of Willie's arm round his shoulders. Aware that he had done something really important. And then, he was suddenly able to think about the others. He could sit there and watch the pattern of all their lives changing. And one pattern, a lovely, warm-coloured pattern, neatly finished.

Cissie died very peacefully before nine o'clock.

There was a subdued flurry of hugs, and words and phone calls, there were tearful smiles in the kitchen and quiet moments by the bed-settee, there was the doctor again, and finally there were the undertakers, quietly, tactfully capable, there was a covering, a lifting and a carrying away, and there was an empty sitting-room.

Mina and Gail stripped the sheets and pillows, put things in the washing-machine, and tidied away the duvet. Stewart and Eric folded back the bed-settee.

Everyone else would be back next day sometime. Eric and Dad were on their own. They walked across the path.

Tomorrow Dad and John would go to town to make the funeral arrangements. Eric would go too; he wouldn't be left at home this time. It wasn't a job that needed three people, it was just something that men always did, and he had to see.

When they came into their own kitchen, it was half-past twelve, and years since morning, but it was impossible to sleep. They looked at each other.

Willie said, "Wid du laek a gless o whisky, Eric?"

Well, well.

"I'd redder hae a beer, please."

Eric plugged in the fan heater. They sat down by the table, companions. For a few minutes they sipped their drinks in silence.

Then Eric said, before he lost courage, "Dad, I wid need ta tell dee aboot Friday night."

Shetland Black
—————————————————— Chapter 20 ——————————————————

Meg, Monday Morning

On Monday morning, Whalvoe was black calm, the water dark with reflected steepness. It had rained on the night and the valley was fresh, the air sharp and clear as Meg drove reluctantly to work. Today would not be easy. The sympathy and the speculation would all centre on her neighbours, and she would have to hear it all, monitor it all.

It was not a pleasant feeling. And the worst of it was, the thing wasn't finished. There was still a body on a post-mortem list somewhere in Aberdeen, and the results would not be known till at least tonight, maybe tomorrow.

Cissie was gone, and that she needed time to believe. And Cissie had taken Eric for Davie. Meg had cried when she heard it, and Evan had held her and asked her why.

Evan had stayed, of course. He'd only just left. Tonight was his last night ashore for a fortnight. She could hardly expect him to come over again, though. She would be getting to depend on him.

Meg sighed as she stopped the car and stepped out to greet the postmen. The mail van came into sight. The day began as expected.

Monday morning was usually quiet, and Annie Brown didn't start work till eleven. Meg found the familiar shop routine like a refuge. The freezers hummed, the place looked neat and bright. She dusted, re-arranged and stocked shelves with a will, and was all calm efficiency with the early customers, who were mostly on their way to work and stopping in for cigarettes or petrol. After nine o'clock, there was a lull.

At half past nine, she phoned Mary.

"I'm just phonin ta say foo sorry I am aboot Cissie. I'll miss her a lock."

She wondered if Mary would talk to her today. Wondered if Mary might have come along her last night, if Evan's car hadn't been outside the house.

"Tanks ta dee, Meg. It wis very paeceful, du kens."

She sounded calm, at least, and not so distant as yesterday. Fewer tablets, perhaps.

"Are dey onything du's needin, Mary, at I could tak hame?"

"Oh, Guid kens. Yes, dey laekly are, dat wid be fine." She thought of several things. "Will du be ower, dan?"

"Yes, yes, I'll be ower when I come hame."

"Dat's fine."

The door bell rang while Meg was fetching milk from the back shop chill cabinet. She didn't recognise the green Fiesta outside.

Marilyn Thompson was standing hesitantly just inside the door, looking all round, very uncertain.

"Meg, I towt I wid maybe better come alang. Foo is Cissie? I heard she wis hed a stroke."

Meg put down the case of milk. "She's no livin. She deed da streen."

Marilyn's face fell and she burst into tears.

A Land Rover full of hydro men drew up at the petrol pumps. Meg took Marilyn by the arm, led her into the back shop and found her a chair.

When Meg returned from the shop, Marilyn was still crying. Meg switched on the kettle and made coffee. By and by, the lass was calmer. She accepted coffee and a biscuit, and then lit up a cigarette.

Meg found it very hard to know what to say, but finally said, "Can I help in ony wye?"

Shake of blonde head. "No!" she raised her eyes. "Du kens, doesn' du? Jacqueline most a telled dee. I left yesterday. I'm at Amy's. I'm no goin back ageen."

"Is du sure?"

"Bloody right!" She drew hard on the cigarette. "He widna want me anywye."

No words came to Meg.

"But anywye," Marilyn went on, "dat's no what I cam ta spaek aboot. Jacqueline spak ta me late on da streen, an she said aboot Cissie. I kent she wis wantin ta fin oot aboot da New Zealand boy, but I never kent why, till Jacqueline said. I never kent it wis dat important, Meg. I towt du might be able ta tell her."

"Tell her?"

"He said his graandmidder cam fae da Wastside. Her whole faimily emigrated. His faider's folk wis fae Greenock."

"So he wis nae relation?"

Marilyn shook her head. It was quiet in the back shop.

"Wis she awful upset aboot it, Meg?" Marilyn's voice shook.

Meg put a hand on her arm and spoke as firmly as she could. "It wisna dy faat. It wis just an unlucky chance. An onywye, hit wrought oot winderful in da end."

She managed to tell it, though it wasn't easy.

After a few moments, Marilyn asked, "How did Eric cope?"

"Very weel, I tink."

"Poor Eric," said Marilyn, staring at the floor. "He's dat young."

Someone came into the shop. Meg rose hastily to look.

"Oh, it's dee, Erty. I'll be oot in a meenit."

"Nae hurry, lass. Tak du dee tay."

Marilyn rose.

"Weel," said Meg, "tanks ta dee for comin, an bein sae concerned. Du could just a phoned."

Stubbed cigarette. "I wis comin by anywye. I'm goin ta spaek ta Jack."

"You'll maybe sort it oot."

"Na." She looked at Meg. "He wis a fine craiter ta spaek tae. He maybe did intend ta come alang me. But he never cam. An I didna bloody ax him tae edder. Jack winna believe me. He tinks I'm tellin lies because I never mentioned giein da boy a lift." Her voice grew louder. "Of coorse I never mentioned it! I never mentioned it because I wis fairt at he wid *tink* at I wis invited him ower. I never mentioned it ta onybody at all for dat very sam raison. Dey wid aa a jumpit ta da sam conclusion!"

Erty, shuffling round the shop, began to whistle "The Girl I left Behind Me."

Marilyn gave a bitter smile. "I tink I'll dye my head broon."

Meg showed her to the back door. She turned on the step.

"Anidder thing at's been budderin me," she said. "Da boy's pals is in Foula. Does du tink dey'll be heard, or wid we need ta get wird ta dem?"

"Pals?"

"Yes, dey were tree o dem. Da idder twa fell mad ta go ta Foula for da weekend, but he didna fancy da sea journey, so he cam here. What does du tink, Meg? I tink dey come back again da moarn. What should I do?"

Two boys, coming carefree off the Foula ferry tomorrow . . .

"I suppose," said Meg hesitantly, "du could laekly tell da sergeant. Just in case. Dey'll maybe no be heard, oot in Foula. Wid — wid du laek me ta tell him?"

"No, I'll tell him mesell. I should a telled him afore. It maks nae difference noo."

Her face was bleak. She looked much older.

Meg said, "Mind, someen idder maybe kent aboot da boy's pals. Dey're maybe been telled already."

"Weel, maybe." She was leaving.

"Marilyn!" Head turn. "Jack'll maybe believe dee. Because he will want ta believe dee. You aye dö — *want* ta believe."

She looked, then shrugged her shoulders. "Cheerio, Meg. Thanks for da coffee — an dee time."

Meg leaned against the door and felt sick at heart.

Erty was cheery as always, and Meg was thankful to see him. She was only sorry she felt obliged to tell him about Cissie.

Shetland Black

―――――――――――――― **Chapter 21** ――――――――――――――

Donald and Mary, Monday Morning

Donald woke at ten o'clock and did not know what day it was, but his head was clear and the world in sharp focus. His hands, as he pulled on clothes, did not shake too much. It looked a dry day.

He wondered if Mary was out; he heard no sound. He'd grill some bacon and make toast and a pot of tea. See what there was in the fridge.

He had a quick shower, and felt clean.

Then the kitchen, and Mary there, and finding out it was Monday, and remembering.

And the old wife had died. She was dead. Cissie, gone. While he slept.

It was a clear morning, a calm day. There was work to do. It couldn't be true, all this; it must be a dream. And the policeman, the camper, the dent in the van, maybe they were part of the dream.

Donald sat stunned at the kitchen table and ate bread. The tea in the pot was old and too long brewed, but he drank it.

"So der naething I can dö, dan," he eventually said.

"No. Dey aa guid ta Lerook a while ago."

"Weel dan, I'll geng doon ta da pier."

He left, chair scraping on vinyl, door slamming. The outdoor light was harsh; his feet seemed to echo on the paving stones. He could see the dent in the van from the doorstep.

Mary washed his dirty cup and put it back on the rack.

The sun was shining in the back windows. Sunshine fairly showed up dirty windows. She ought to be outside washing them down. Salt in the air, that was the problem.

There was so much she ought to be doing, but it didn't seem right today. Mam said you had to have respect for the dead.

Mam would never know. She wouldn't be looking again with those searching eyes that missed nothing. There would be no more half-questions, no more sideways glances when she thought you didn't notice, no more need for swift changes of subject, no more probing.

It was a big mistake to live so near your mother. There was no privacy. She would always feel responsible for you, always need to know.

She would not know now. She was spared that. Mary was spared that.

Meg would be over tonight. Joanne would phone tonight for sure; she'd have found Mary's message on her machine by now.

Joanne might want to come home for the funeral. Mary would make it clear there was no need for that. Far too far, too hard for her to get away. Nobody was expecting her to come. Send flowers, Joanne. Come home in summer-time. Not now.

There had been no word from Chris since last Tuesday's letter. If she didn't phone tonight, Mary would have to try the emergency number in the nurses' home. But if she hadn't phoned, it probably meant she wasn't there.

A car engine started up outside. Sandy the postman turned out from the side of the house and headed out the road. She hadn't heard him arrive.

On the porch mat were three letters. Two were for Donald, but Mary hardly saw them, and never knew where she laid them down, because the top one, with the first-class stamp, was from Chris.

Shetland Black

--------------------------------- Chapter 22 ---------------------------------

Monday Afternoon

The expected phone call from Lerwick came at twelve o'clock. Meg noted the details, duly wrote out the black-edged funeral notice, and fixed it to the shop door. The funeral of the late Christina Mary Hendry would take place on Wednesday at two p.m. Christina Mary looked wrong; Meg added brackets and wrote CISSIE in capital letters. It still looked wrong. Funeral notices always looked wrong, if you had to write them.

Eric sat in the back of John's car in a Lerwick car park and thought about coffins, brass handles and price lists. Kindly people in an ordinary office with holiday postcards on the walls. The clip of high heels in a stone corridor, an order book, a ringing telephone, a word processor. A shop smelling of green leaves, apologies because it was Monday, pictures of flowers, another order book. "Will it be *In Loving Memory* or *With Sincere Sympathy?*" More prices. Biro pen. And in a cold quiet room, a white-clad body rigidly straight on a draped table, eyes closed. Willie and John had each laid a hand on the creamy pale forehead, and he had felt obliged to follow suit. He had dreaded it, but it had shown him something. The skin was cold and dry, the face hard bones. This you could put in the ground, it wasn't Granny. If he had only been brave enough to look at Mam, he would have known this before.

You had to face up to things, whatever happened.

John returned to the car with fish suppers. Suddenly, Eric was achingly hungry. While they ate, the men discussed the question of pall-bearers. "Wis tree, an wha idder?"

Donald ate his dinner at a great speed and rose to his feet, stepping over the remains of the tattie dish Mary had just dropped and broken.

"I'll hae ta be gyaain. Need ta win ta Lerook."

He'd be through Brugafirth and out the other side while most folk were still at the dinner table. He had enough petrol to take him to Lerwick, no need to stop at Meg's.

He did have yon appointment at half-past two at the Advice place. But that could wait till another day. He'd ring later and explain there had been a death in the family.

By two, he was in the town. He drove past the Supersave and the shopping centre, where you were very likely to meet folk you knew. Instead, he parked beside a licensed grocer's in a side street. He'd been there once or twice before.

He came to the counter with an array of bottles, and two pints of milk for the house. In front of him was an elderly woman. When he heard her north mainland voice, he stood back a little and turned his face aside, but as she picked up her shopping, she looked his way. To his horror, he recognised her as Nessie Clark's mother, Lizzie. She had moved to the town to stay with her other daughter a couple of years back. She had been friendly with Cissie.

"My mercy," Lizzie said, "is dis dee, Donald? Isn' dat queer? I wis just hearin fae wir Nessie at Cissie is no livin. I'm truly awful vexed ta hear it. Foo is Mary, poor lass?"

Damn the woman. Just his luck to meet her.

"Oh weel," he said, "she's no sae bad. Aa da wye at she can be, du kens." He couldn't for the life of him remember how Mary was.

Lizzie let him in to the till, but stood still, compelling him to set all his purchases on the counter before her. She seemed taken up with her thoughts and did not look at them.

"An Nessie wis sayin tö aboot yon poor boy fae New Zealand at dey fan at Litlagill. Are dey ever fun oot if he *wis* ony freend ta Cissie?"

He stared at her.

"Oh my," she said, colouring a little, "I maybe wisna meant ta repeat dat."

The total on the till was bloody unbelievable. He scrabbled in pockets for his cheque-book. What was this shite she was saying?

"Whaar ta hell did du hear dat, wumman? What'n shite you do spaek!"

The shop assistant, waiting for the cheque, began to look embarrassed.

"Weel," said Lizzie, surprised and offended, "du needna be sae nesty aboot it." She surveyed his shopping with a sharp noticing eye. "Jessie Anderson wis phonin all ower da place on Setterday night ta fin folk at wis spokken ta dis boy, because Cissie wis fairt at since his name wis Pearson, he might a been a graandson o her bridder Davie's, him at jamp ship in Wellington. Dat's da truth. She maybe never axed *dee*," she paused with a meaningful look at the drink, "but whedder dey were a connection or no, hit's nae lee at I'm tellin, I can assure dee!"

The shop door clanged as Lizzie went out.

All the way home he racked his brains to remember what he could of Terry Pearson on Friday night. There was something, something he ought to mind . . .

He took the old road through Tingwall, hauled off on to the verge at the quiet loch of Vatster and broke into the vodka. He had almost remembered . . .

". . . *yeh, roots, thet's it. Most Kiwis do it, sooner or lyter . . .*"

". . . *not at its best just now, I guess, but I always heard it can be beautiful . . .*"

". . . *well, a quarter-Shetlander, anywye. Cheers!*"

The boy had told him, hadn't he? And wouldn't he have asked him questions? Wouldn't he have said, "Where did your folk come from?" He had said that, hadn't he? And what had Terry Pearson replied?

Had he said, "*My grendfather came from hereabouts. My grendfather's name was David Pearson*"? Was that what he had said? Donald could imagine him saying that. Maybe he had said it.

The boy had reminded him a bit of Eric. He could definitely remember that. Donald broke out in a sweat.

John drew up at Meg's shop. None of them mentioned the funeral notice on the door. A couple of elderly people leaving the shop spied them and stopped.

"Eric," said Willie, "wid du geng in an buy something for da tay? Better lay in some extra bread an mylk." He reached into his pocket for money, but Eric forestalled him.

"It's aa right. I hae money." He got out. The waiting couple advanced hesitantly to greet the brothers. "Boys, we were sorry ta hear . . ."

Sympathy again. They'd already met some in Lerwick. But he could bear it this time, Eric thought. He could feel the kindness in it, could appreciate the regret. It was a support, after all, he could see that now.

There was never much meat in the chill cabinet on Mondays, and Eric resorted to the freezers. In the next aisle, two unseen women were deep in conversation.

". . . anidder twa! It's everywye you look!"

"It's a shame, an dat peerie boy hardly a year aald."

"He wis aye awful jealous o her, dey mean ta say."

"Weel, maybe no athoot caase . . ."

Eric retrieved two microwave meals from the bottom of a freezer, and moved on to the bacon and the milk. The voices were nearer.

"An dis wis aa ower dis New Zealander?"

Eric stood still.

"Yes, yes, du sees, Jack surely towt at he wis been veesitin Marilyn, but she denied it."

"Weel, of coorse she wid a denied it! I heard at she wis hed him in da car wi her on Friday. She never said aboot dat ta naebody edder. Believe du me, der been something."

"Weel, I never ken da lass at all, but onywye, she's surely left him an cleared oot ta someen she kens in Scallowa."

"Dear a dear. What'll we be hearin next?"

Eric waited till the two of them were out the door, then hurried to the check-out. Thank God, it was Meg on the till. He accepted her kind words for him, though he hardly heard them.

"Meg, " he said urgently, "is yon right at Bessie an Janette wis sayin, at Marilyn is left Jack?"

Meg sighed. "Yes, Eric, it is right, I'm sorry ta say."

"An it wis because o da New Zealand boy?"

"Weel, seeminly so. But Marilyn says dat's no true."

"It's no true, Meg. I ken it's no true!"

Meg looked at him in surprise.

"Is Marilyn in Scallowa, laek dey were sayin?"

"Yes. She wis here dis moarnin, an dat's what she said."

"How wis she?"

Meg hesitated. "Braaly shakken up."

Eric seized his carrier bag. "Thanks, Meg," he said, and rushed to the door.

Shetland Black

——————————— Chapter 23 ———————————

Monday Evening, Donald and Meg

Donald sat in his salmon feed store and surveyed the sea through the window. It was a fine night, but there was a breeze setting up from the south-west. Tomorrow morning it would be lying right in the voe.

It was teatime. It was well past teatime. Mary would be getting mad with him. Well, let her wait. She deserved it. Letting him hear news from strangers. She'd made him look a complete fool. But wasn't that what she thought he was, a complete fool? Never good enough at anything. No brains, no backbone. She treated him like an idiot. When did she ever take a real interest in him? Only when she was afraid he might make an exhibition of himself.

What an exhibition he would make shortly, in the sheriff court. In the paper. What would she say then? Serve her bloody well right. Her and her houseproud fussy ways.

What would the lasses think, though? God, would they have to know? Of course they would have to know. He'd tell them himself, wouldn't let Mary do it. She'd set them against him.

Would he have to go to prison?

Christ, what if the boy was a relation? A tragedy, a bloody tragedy.

He'd give Mary what for, for not telling him the story. Treating him like a bairn. He drained the bottle and got to his feet.

He stood on his kitchen floor and listened. Listened to her saying she never knew, it was the first she'd heard of it, none of them had ever mentioned a word. Damned lies. And then she pretended to get upset, and asked him questions about Terry Pearson — what had he said and what had he asked and did he really look like Eric? And she'd gone on, making a good performance out of it. The most wrought up he'd ever seen her. The tears were even starting to flow. And she kept entreating him to sit down and eat his tea.

Well, he'd soon show her what he thought of her and her tea. He picked up the plate of sausage and egg, walked to the bin, and emptied the lot inside. And good God, there were two letters addressed to him, in the bin, unopened, among the bruck. He seized them, rubbing them clean with a nearby dishcloth, and turned on her.

"An is dis what du does wi my mail?"

He wouldn't stay here a minute longer. He slammed the kitchen door and stood in the porch to open his letters, when the outside door opened, and Meg Inkster came in.

"Weel, Donald," said Meg, "it's a fine night."

He seemed to stare a little, but he spoke affably enough.

"Yes, yes, it is dat. A scaar o wind comin up, though."

"Is Mary in?"

"Oh yes, she's in." He frowned slightly. "Kinda wrought up, though. It's fine du's come. Geng du in."

He looked down at the two envelopes in his hand, and seemed preoccupied. Meg wondered if he was sober. Sometimes it was hard to tell. She opened the kitchen door and went in.

Mary sat on the kitchen sofa, sobbing her heart out.

Meg was honestly relieved. Grief was natural and right. Crying would do Mary a lot more good than doping herself with tablets. Meg set down the box of groceries she was carrying, put an arm around Mary's shoulders and said nothing.

She heard the outside door open and close before Mary managed to say, "Meg, tell me, is it right at da New Zealand boy wis related ta wis?"

Somebody must have said something. Well, at least she could help there.

"No, Mary, I can tell dee definitely at he wisna. I ken dat for a fact. I spak wi someen da day at kent aa aboot him. His faider's folk cam fae Greenock. He did hae a Shetlan graandmidder but she cam fae da Wastside. Dey were nae connection wi you at all."

Mary stared. "Weel, what wye did folk tink at dey might be?"

"It wis just dee midder at kinda got da idea when she heard da boy's name an whaar he cam fae. So dey tried ta fin oot aboot him. An dey never telled dee or Donald because dey never believed it wid be right, and you hed enough on your minds athoot yon. I'm only vexed I didna fin oot da right wye o it shöner."

Mary wiped her eyes. She looked dreadful.

"Is dis been on dee mind aa day?"

"Oh no!" Mary shook her head. "Donald just said aboot it eenoo. He — he heard it in Lerook. He towt I kent an wis never telled him." Her eyes brimmed. "He widna aet his tay!" she whispered, and sobbed again.

Deevil tak him, thought Meg. "Is *du* hed ony tay, Mary?"

Mary looked vague.

"Right!" Meg rose. "I'll mak a cup ta dee. An du can try een o dis new kind o biscuit I'm brought dee."

She tried to chat, but it was difficult. So many topics seemed to lead somehow to Terry Pearson. Yes, Willie had looked along to tell Mary about the funeral arrangements. Yes, some folk had phoned. Yes, John and Mina would be coming along sometime tonight.

"An is du spokken ta da lasses?"

"Joanne phoned at six. She's awful vexed, an sorry she canna mak it ta da funeral. Dey're dat short-staffed, an she can hardly get time aff at short notice, no in her position."

Silence. Meg handed Mary a cup of tea, then took it back, the hands were shaking so much.

"Mary, what is it?"

The eyes were dark and ashamed. "It's Chris. She's haein ta gie up nursin."

"What's happened?"

"She's — she's gyaain ta hae a bairn." The voice died to a whisper.

"Oh. Weel, dat's no really such'n a terrible thing nooadays. No laek it used ta be."

"She's never feenished her trainin."

"Dat's a peety, right enough. But she'll surely be able ta feenish it trow time."

"I dönna ken."

"Foo does she feel aboot it hersell?"

"She guid awa tae a pal o hers for twartree days ta mak up her mind what ta dö, an noo she says she's gyaain ta hae da bairn an keep it."

"Weel, dat's her decision, Mary. Du'll hae ta accept dat."

Mary stared at the floor and said, almost venomously, "I tink she sood a gotten clear o it! It's no as if it wid be hard, nooadays!"

Meg, shocked, said "Oh *Mary*! How could du say dat?"

"She's been goin wi a mairried man! She's wrought no sense at all! All da chances she's hed, efter everything at I'm done for her!"

Meg, who had never met Chris, was thrown back on Cissie's description — *headstrong, owersteer, but guid-herted*. She listened in silence to a bitter description of Mary's wayward daughter. Mary was distracted. She couldn't mean half the things she was saying.

"An she'll never manage on her ain! She'll laekly come laandin hame apo me!" Mary shook her head. "I'm truly blyde at Mam doesna hae ta ken aboot dis! She's weel oot o it!"

Meg was at a loss. "What does Donald say?"

Mary raised her eyes. "Donald?" Her face took on a different look. "Donald? I'm no telled him yet. But he'll just want her hame. She could never dö wrang in his eyes."

Meg decided to brave it.

"An foo *is* Donald, Mary?"

The eyes dropped, the head turned away. Mary leaned away from her and straightened the sofa cushions.

"He's . . ."

She eyed something on the floor by her feet and picked it up. It was a fragment of Pyrex glass. She held it between her fingers and looked at it, frowning. Then she looked at Meg.

"He's braaly . . . worried."

"Worried." Meg nodded encouragingly. "Of coorse."

Nothing more. Wait. Wait. Mary turned the shiny little white jag of glass over and over. Meg wanted to reach out and take it from her.

"Du sees," said Mary at last," he's ower 50, an he might no get anidder job if dey dönna keep him on."

This was not what Meg had been thinking of, but of course it was true. Another burden on them.

"Whan'll he ken?"

"He's aye lippenin wird. Aye lookin for da mail."

She sat up and gaped at Meg. "Oh! Da letters!"

The letters lay among the hyacinths on the porch window-sill, torn envelopes beside them. One was an invoice, the other on headed notepaper. Mary seized it and read.

"He's paid aff!" she said loudly. "Dey're no wantin him! Oh Meg, Meg, whaar is he *geen*?"

There was blood on her fingers, and terror in her face.

Shetland Black

—————————————— Chapter 24 ——————————————

Willie, Monday Evening

Willie was waiting impatiently, but tried to hide the fact behind the *Radio Times*.

"Weel," he said, as Eric came in, "foo did du get on?"

Eric took off his jacket. "Aa right. Hamish just got hame, so I'm spokken tae him for a start an gotten things cleared up." He eyed the tea table, looked in the microwave, and switched it on.

"Der nae mair wird fae da sergeant?"

"He's never been ta see Hamish. An naebody's heard ony wird o da post-mortem result yet. Hit'll maybe no come for da moarn."

"Weel," said Willie, "der nae need o dee döin ony mair eenoo. Just laeve it till we see what happens."

"Yes, Dad." The microwave gave a *ping*. "Dat's what du keeps sayin." He took out the shepherd's pie and sat down to the table. He didn't look convinced.

"If du tries ta spaek ta Jack Thompson," said Willie, his heart in his mouth, "du's just as laekly ta mak things werr, no better!"

"Yes, I ken dat. I ken dat!" Eric gave Willie one of the new direct looks he seemed to favour. "It's just at — weel — I feel dat awful aboot it, Dad."

He wasn't so old, after all, however mature he seemed suddenly to have become. Willie hoped for a favourable outcome to the post-mortem, though in his heart he felt it was unlikely.

It was not twenty-four hours since Cissie died, and already it seemed like a month ago, he was so worried about Eric. But there was no need to let Eric see that. He nodded gently, and rose to start washing up.

"We'll better get dis tay cleared awa," he said, "afore Mina comes in."

Eric groaned. "I dönna hae ta sit here wi her, do I? Hamish said he wid come ower efter, if I wis clear."

"I tink," said Willie, "we'll maybe lat dee escape." Eric looked up with a surprised flicker of a grin.

The phone rang at Willie's side.

"Willie?" It was Meg. "Willie, could dee or Eric hae a look an see if Donald is doon at da pier?"

She sounded strange. Before he could answer, he heard Mary's voice in the background, high-pitched.

"It's Mary at's anxious ta ken whaar he is. He's taen da van."

"Aa right. Is du at Mary's?"

"Yes, yes, I'm dere. Could du just come alang?"

"An what if he is dere, Meg? What am I ta say tae him?"

"Say nothing! Just see if he's dere."

Mary's voice cried, "Tell him ta hurry up!"

"Right. Cheerio."

"What's happenin, Dad?"

Willie reached into the cupboard for his jacket. "Donald is geen a-missin an Mary is panickin. He'll be on da booze. I'm ta look an see if he's doon at da pier. Weel, at laest she's hed da sense no ta trail efter him hersell. Dat really *does* set him high."

"Is he *drivin*?"

"Yea, yea, he haes da van. I'll laekly be expected ta do a commando raid an tak her hame. But dat's *all* I'm doin. If he's at da pier, he can walk hame. If he's ony idder wye, he can get a taxi. If it comes ta takkin *Donald* hame, I'm no even goin ta try. He'll no geng till he's ready." He made for da door.

"I'm comin too."

"Weel, weel, come if du wants."

The pier was deserted, cold water slapping round stanchions. The store was shut. No sign of the van.

Mary met them at the door, face flushed, eyes piercing. "Is he dere? Der nae sign o him? Are you sure?"

Willie said, "Will he no be at da pub?"

Meg said "Yes, yes, he'll be at da pub." She looked at Willie meaningfully.

"I'll phone Bob Tulloch!" said Mary, and left the kitchen.

Meg said urgently, "She's in a terrible state! Donald is just heard at he's no bein keepit on at da salmon. He's been on da drink da day already, an she's fairt what he'll do. He wis surely in a terrible mood even afore he fan dis oot — an he's drivin, of coorse. She's just oot o her head. I hed a job persuadin her no ta geng lookin for him hersell."

"Thank God du pat her aff o dat," said Willie with feeling. "I'll never forget last Christmas!"

"Weel, could you geng an look for him?"

"Yea, we'll geng. But Meg, du kens, we might be safer ta laeve him whaar he is, as lang as we tak da van hame."

"Poor Donald!" said Eric suddenly. They looked at him.

"He most feel just hellish!"

"Weel, of coorse," said Meg quietly. "Du's right, Eric. He's a feelin-herted craiter, hit *is* hellish for him. But du kens, he can get terrible tirn wi a drink in. An him drivin . . ." Her words trailed away into a little silence.

Then Mary burst into the kitchen. "He's dere! He's at da pub! We'll go an get him hom!"

"No, no, Mary!" Meg took her firmly by the arm. "It's no needin wis aa ta go. Willie an Eric is goin. Donald widna laek it if we guid."

The men went out to the pick-up. Meg stepped after them, closing the door behind her.

"Willie, I tink I'm gyaain ta hae ta try an get some o yon tablets ta Mary. She's run oot o dem, an when she phoned for mair dis morning, dey said she hed ta see da doctor first, an of coorse she didna want ta geng ta da surgery among da folk, so she never guid. But I tink I sood phone da doctor himsell an try an get some tablets for her. She can hardly dö athoot dem. No eenoo."

Mary opened the door. "Hurry up!" she screamed. "Dönna hinder dem, Meg!"

"Phone da doctor, Meg," said Willie, starting up. "I'll fetch da bloody tablets fae Lerook if I hae tae. Da wumman is crackin up."

They didn't speak, all the way to Brugafirth. Eric looked towards the empty Roselea drive.

There were only a few cars at the pub, Donald's van among them. Willie drove up round the corner, out of sight of the bar windows.

"Weel, first things first. I'll tak da van hame. Du could maybe geng in an see what'n a state he's in. He'll no staand aff o dee laek he wid o

77

me. Dan du can come hame an lat me ken. If he's döin nae faat, we'll just laeve him ta come hame himsell. Da important thing is not ta mak him tirn."

Eric was tense. "OK. I'll just mak on I'm lookin for Hamish." They parted company.

Willie opened the van door and swore.

"What is it, Dad?"

"Da keys!" said Willie, looking all round the driver's seat. "He's taen da bloody keys!"

Shetland Black

—————————— Chapter 25 ——————————

Bob Tulloch

B ob Tulloch put down the phone and headed back into the public bar. There wasn't much for Kathy Bruce to do in the lounge end tonight, but she'd be better there. She should never have served Donald in the first place, but she didn't know him like Bob did. Didn't have so much to lose either.

There he was, still unsteadily feeding the juke-box with coins that rattled to the floor every now and again. He hadn't finished his pint, but the second double nip was long gone.

Poor bugger, why couldn't he just go? He was making the others uncomfortable. Shouting for Tammy Sinclair, bursting into wild laughter, demanding loud music, staggering into dance. If he would only sit still, it wouldn't be so bad. Even Jim o Braeview was finding him an embarrassment.

The wife had sounded hysterical on the phone. But he wouldn't mention that. Nothing would be less likely to send Donald home.

It took Bob one moment of surprise to figure out that young Eric Hendry's arrival was a planned manoeuvre, but not supposed to look like one. Well, he would play along.

"Aye, aye, Eric," he said, quite business-like. "An what can I get dee da night? Foo is your folk at Clivagarth? I wis awful sorry aboot dee graandmidder."

"Thanks, Bob," said the boy, sitting on a stool and looking casually around. "Dey're no sae bad. I'll hae a half a lager. Are you seen Hamish aboot?"

Hamish was not normally aboot on a Monday night either, but Bob replied with great confidence, "Oh, he'll laekly be comin. If du just hings on a moment, he'll laekly be in." He served up Eric's lager.

Eric was doing well. He hadn't paid any attention to Donald at all. You might even have thought he was hoping Donald wouldn't notice him.

Donald had. He slouched up alongside and slapped the boy on the shoulder. "Well, it's peerie Eric! Boy, boy! Have a dram fae dee owld uncle!"

"Na tanks," said Eric. "I hae a lager here. I'll hae een fae dee efter. How's du doin, Uncle Donald?"

"Oh splendid, splendid, man!" Donald sat down on an empty stool and banged his pint on the bar. "Bright lights, good music an good company! What more could you want, eh?" He turned to the man on his other side. "What more could you want, Jim? What more, what more? Dönna be sae bloody soor, man!" He swivelled back to Eric. "Here's a man at kens how ta have a good time. Eighteen! Boy, I wiss I wis eighteen."

Bob was trying to stay at a distance, but he saw the shadow cross Eric's face. Yet the boy replied cheerily, "Me an Hamish is awey ta Lerook da night. We're goin ta da Thule."

"Da Thule?" Donald took a swig of beer. "Boy, it's a long while fae I wis at da Thule last."

"Weel, du can come wi wis if du wants. I'm goin along for Hamish eenoo. It'll be a fun. Is du comin? Dey'll be plenty o folk dere at'll ken dee."

Bob held his breath.

"Weel — I maybe will. Go on da town."

A caustic old voice spoke up from a nearby table. "In wir day, I tink we widna a geen rantin ta da pubs wi a graandmidder hardly cowld."

It took an effort, but Eric ignored it. A murmur of disgust rose from the other men. Old Jeemie rose from his table, went out and closed the door emphatically.

"Weel," said Eric, getting up, "will we go, dan?"

Donald drained his glass and rose. The juke box began to play "By the Rivers of Babylon". Donald started to sing and do little dance steps over the lino tiles. Then he clasped Eric around the neck and they made jauntily for the door.

Old Jeemie came in from the passage. He'd only been at the toilet. He looked disapprovingly at Eric.

"Dee faider is here wi da pick-up ta fetch dee."

Without batting an eye, Eric said "Oh na, yon's me. I'm drivin da pick-up."

Donald released his grip on Eric's shoulders and looked at him. Then he said "Excuse me a meenit, boy. I'll hae ta geng whaar Jeemie is been." He waved a hand towards the other end of the bar. "Wid du tak my kep?" And out he went.

Eric fairly ran to the far end of the bar and looked. Others looked too.

"Whaar's dis kep?"

"Kep? He didna hae a kep."

"He wears a black kep."

"I see nae kep."

"He hed no kep, I'm tellin dee!"

"It's just a ploy, Eric!"

Outside, a van engine roared.

"He's gone!" said Eric, and rushed from the bar.

The men turned slowly back to their drinks.

"Poor Eric!" said Jim o Braeview. "He did weel."

"Could du no a held dy jaas?" said Andrew to Old Jeemie. "Yon wis aa a stunt ta get Donald oot o here. Da boy wis döin his best."

"Weel," said Bob heavily, "da police'll laekly meet him. I phoned dem ten meenits ago an axed dem ta look ower."

Six pairs of eyes looked at him.

"Boys, what idder could I dö, efter Friday? I couldna a served him ageen. I wis goin ta hae ta pit him oot. I wis fairt what happened."

Silence.

"It's my licence, boys! It's aa right for you!"

They knew that. They understood. He could see that in the eyes. He could also see the relief that there were none of them in his shoes.

Shetland Black

———————————— **Chapter 26** ————————————

Monday Evening

Eric and Willie reached the top of the hill of Brugafirth, which overlooked the loch of Houbister and the Houbister juction.

"Now look an see if he maks for Tammie Sinclair's." Willie drew off on to the verge of the road. "If he goes dere, he'll bide, an maybe faa asleep. I'll phone Tammie ta tak da rotor airm aff o da van and dan he'll win nae farder. I wiss I wid a done dat at da pub."

Eric stiffened. "Dad, here's da police comin! On da idder side o da loch!"

Below them, Donald's van reached the Houbister junction. It spun round and set off back towards them.

"God," said Willie, "he surely will mak for hom noo."

Eric said, "Maybe dis is da post-mortem result come trow." His face was white.

Once Donald had passed them, Willie turned around. The police car was now out of sight in the bends of the road, but they were all heading north. It was starting to rain.

"I think, Mrs Jamieson," the doctor said, "I'll give you an injection. It'll help you to feel calmer, and possibly sleep."

"I'm no wantin ta sleep!" Mary sat up in the sofa. "Foo can I sleep till I ken what's happenin?"

"Du'll no sleep eenoo, Mary," said Meg anxiously. "But it'll help dee ta sleep later *on*."

The needle hovered.

"It's just laek dee tablets. Isn' it, doctor?"

"Just much the same, yes."

Then John and Mina came in, at the wrong moment.

Evan Ritchie rang Meg's number for the third time in an hour.

Marilyn settled Martin to sleep in Amy's spare room and wondered about Jack. He'd seemed so quiet, both times she'd seen him. And so upset at leaving Martin just now. But he hadn't shown any signs of remorse. And in her mind, she could still hear what he'd called her. She would always hear it.

Jack, meantime, was nearing home after his visit to Scalloway. He drove quite slowly. There was no need to rush home to an empty house. Yet there was nowhere else he felt like going.

Martin seemed to have forgotten yesterday morning. He had been so afraid the peerie boy would be scared of him. He wasn't; he had smiled and cuddled and been delighted, as usual. They had spent a good half-hour in Amy's sitting-room.

Marilyn had said little; he'd hardly seen her. Perhaps *she* was afraid of him. Perhaps she felt guilty. Perhaps Amy had got at her.

Amy made him feel like the lowest of the low. It was amazing how she could do it, with only the fewest of words. Even when she opened the door.

"Oh," she'd said. "It's *dee*. Just wait a meenit, will du?" It was the tone of voice that got you.

He couldn't talk to Marilyn without Amy listening. It was a wonder she hadn't come to Roselea with her in the morning. Clearly she regretted the move; something had been said in his hearing . . . "no, du's not ta go on dee own again." It made him feel like a criminal.

Damn it, he hadn't laid a finger near her. What right had Amy to make him feel so guilty? She was nothing but a hard-faced, interfering bitch!

He drew up outside Roselea and began to reverse in the drive. He was in the middle of this manoeuvre when a van appeared through the rain at speed. Jack accelerated, but the van, charging ahead, ran straight into the Audi's right wing and sandwiched the car against the gatepost. There was a crunching and a bending of metal, and Jack's right headlamp burst into fragments.

Jarred by the shock, Jack stalled the engine. The van drew back, allowing him to see behind the wheel the staring face of Donald Jamieson. Then it lurched out into the road and shot off on its way.

The right front wheel could still turn, somehow. Enraged, Jack started up his damaged car and raced after Donald.

Willie and Eric, not far behind, found the glass on the road.

The bloody fool! The crazy bloody fool! He ought to be locked up. He would be, shortly. He just hadn't seen Jack at all. One second sooner, and he'd have hit the driver's door, hit *him*.

Just wait! He'd catch him before he got to the house. No, he wasn't going to the house. The pier, then. The drink store, no doubt!

The man would have bottles everywhere. And he put on such a fine fellow act. At least the family was grown up and gone, but God help his wife. God help her! The damage, the lies, the covering-up, the remorse, the whole thing all over again — Jack knew it. Didn't want to know. Didn't want to think about it.

The van had stopped, the man had got out. He was going to the salmon boat. The *boat*! Stupid bloody typical. He was in no condition for a boat. He was casting off!

Jack stopped right on the pier and jumped out. The man never looked back. The engine was going and he was heading out to the sea. Thirty yards, fifty yards . . . He was standing up in the stern, moving around. He was a crazy man, he'd slip . . .

At the side of the pier was a skiff, with oars. Jack was in it before he could think. As he untied it, he looked around. The salmon boat was heading away on a curve to the right, but it was empty.

When he came near the spot, panting for breath, a bulk was sinking in the water. Jack shed his shoes and his jacket and dived in. It was shockingly, grippingly cold.

And all he could feel was fury. Sheer blazing fury that he should be here, having to do this, of all things, when he could hardly sort out his own problems.

He took a hold of the sinking man's arms and pulled him upwards. At the surface, rain on his wet face, he gasped for air. The man spluttered, struggled, freed an arm, spun round and took a swing at Jack, hitting him full in the face.

Then Jack understood.

"Wid du, du bastard!" he cried in pain, raised his right fist and laid Donald cold.

Then he cradled his head all the way to the shore. He was aware of Willie and Eric helping him get Donald up on to the pier, and aware of a police car.

Shetland Black

——————— **Chapter 27** ———————

Meg, Later Monday Evening

Doctor Macintyre was usually brusque, and not renowned as particularly sociable, but he was willing to sit for a little, and have the cup of tea Meg had suggested. He was a thorough and efficient man; perhaps he wanted to see the effect of the injection on Mary. It was obviously starting to work. The hysteria was gone, and she busied herself manfully with cups and biscuits, though she was still anxious, and kept looking at the clock.

Mina was gallantly making conversation, describing at length the alterations currently being made to their local hall. Mary was nodding; she'd even asked a question. The doctor finished his tea, thanked Mary, and took his leave. She saw him courteously to the door, then turned again with the biscuit plate to John.

Meg rose. "I'm gyaain ta nip hame for a meenit, Mary, an look ta my fire. I'll be back in a moment."

It was raining outside, and she had no jacket. She stepped hurriedly across the turning-place after the doctor. Surely he would need to come along Mary in the morning again, just to keep an eye on her.

Just as the doctor turned to speak, Willie Hendry's pick-up turned in off the road and drew to a swift stop at her side, followed closely by Eric, driving Donald's van. The van had a damaged left wing.

Willie jumped out. "Doctor! Can you hing on a meenit an hae a look at Donald?" And Willie and Eric were opening the van back doors, and the doctor was looking in and frowning, and they were lifting, lifting carefully and pulling Donald out, and he was soaking wet, his green jumper black with wet, his trousers dripping, and his eyes were closed.

Meg leaned along the doctor's car and thought she was going to be sick.

Willie looked at her. "Meg, we'll hae ta tak him ben an tak aff o him an get him waarm. Try ta keep Mary calm. We'll say he slippit ower da pier."

"Is he aa right?" Meg's mouth was dry. She ran to the door after them.

"He's ower weel. We'll tell dee efter." They bundled Donald into the house.

Behind Meg, a door banged. A tall young policeman came striding across from a white police car. The turning place was full of cars.

"Is this the doctor?" Doctor Macintyre turned in the doorway. "Could you have a quick look at another fellow too?"

"Oh bring him in, bring him in. Has he been in the water as well?"

"Fished out the other one." The doctor shook his head and hurried in the door.

"Wha is it?" asked Meg in amazement.

"Name's Jack." The policeman ran back to his car. "Come in, Jack, till the doctor takes a look at you."

"Christ," came Jack Thompson's voice, "I'm no wantin ta come in *here*. Can I no geng hame an get on some dry claes?"

"Doctor says come in."

"I'll fin dee dry claes, Jack, " said Meg, coming to life. "Come in oot o da cowld."

He came in unsteadily, with a policeman's jacket over his shoulders. His face was bruised.

The kitchen was empty. Voices came from ben in the sitting-room. Everyone had followed Donald. Mary was exclaiming and lamenting. Eric could be heard saying "He's aa right! He's just drunk! Jack got a hadd o him!"

Meg took Jack by the arm and showed him into Mary's bathroom. Warm peach-coloured towels hung neatly on a rail. Just beside the bathroom, the airing-cupboard door stood open. There were all sorts of new-aired clothes. Meg snatched jeans, drawers and a jumper.

"Dere," she said. "Staand ida shower, an pit yon on. Gie me oot dee weet claes an I'll pit dem in my washing-machine."

He seemed very weary. "Thanks, Meg."

John and Eric came out of the sitting-room.

"Meg," said John, "wid du fin dem some mair muckle towels, an a pair o breeks or something? We're gyaain ta look for boats."

"Boats?"

"Yes, da salmon boat is nose up alang da banks somewye, an da skiff is driftin."

Eric said, "He jamp oot! I saw him!"

"Shush, Mary'll hear dee."

Meg found towels and trousers and handed them in the ben door. Mary, she thought, had quietened down wonderfully.

There were two black uniforms in the kitchen.

"Oh!"

Of course, they would be waiting to see how Donald was. Her mouth wouldn't smile properly.

The policemen were strangers. They looked slightly uncomfortable. The tall one cleared his throat.

"Er — Mrs Jamieson, is it?"

"Oh, no, no. I'm fae next door." She waved a hand stupidly in the direction of home. "I'm Meg Inkster. Mrs Jamieson — *Mary* — is still lookin efter Donald."

They both nodded.

"He'll surely be all right, will he?"

"Oh, I expect so." Highland accent.

"Lucky chap," said the other policeman. Glaswegian, maybe? Central Belt.

Silence.

"Can I offer you a cup o tay?" Automatic question. They shook their heads. "No, no thank you."

"Cannae drink on the job," the smaller one offered. His partner gave him a look.

All there was to do, then, was sit down.

Meg looked at buttons and braid. Constables, were they? They'd probably met Donald on the road or something. Perhaps he'd taken fright and fled to the pier?

But it was Monday night. The post-mortem result might be through. Perhaps they were here following it up. Would constables do that job?

Surely the sergeant himself would have come, if . . .

She clasped her hands tightly in her lap and sat still. Doctor Macintyre's dark-check coat was slung over a nearby chair. Meg studied every neat interweaving thread.

The silence seemed endless. Presently, Meg could hear the doctor on the phone. He spoke briefly, then knocked on the kitchen door and came in.

"Well," he said, nodding towards the policemen, "he's not too bad, all things considered. But I'm going to put him into hospital for the night, at least. I think he may have a broken jaw as well. Needs an x-ray. Where's the fellow who did the damage? Jack, is it?"

"In da bathroom." Meg rose and knocked on the bathroom door. "Jack, is du aa right? Da doctor is needin ta see dee."

She went back to the kitchen. So Jack had hit Donald. A fight, was it? And then what?

It took the doctor three minutes, right there under the stairs, to pronounce Jack all right. "But don't drive home. Keep warm. Let me know if any dizziness occurs tomorrow. And be careful what you do with that right hand of yours. Lethal weapon!"

It sounded like a joke, but Meg thought Jack Thompson didn't laugh.

"How's Donald?" he said.

Mary came bustling out of the sitting-room.

"Oh Meg," she cried, "Donald haes ta go ta da hospital. I'll hae ta look oot pyjamas an things an pack a bag for him." She came into the kitchen, purposefully, and looked straight into the face of the tall policeman. He rose to his feet.

"Mrs Jamieson. I hope your husband is all right."

Had no-one told Mary the police were here?

Mary stood still and looked slowly from one to the other, then at Meg, then back to the policemen. Mina stood at her back. Willie must still be beside Donald in the sitting-room, the doctor and Jack in the passage.

"Well," said Mary with perfect politeness, "if you're come ta see my husband, he's on his wye ta hospital. I'm sorry, you canna spaek ta him da night."

"Of course not, Mrs Jamieson. We won't be bothering him tonight. I hope he'll be fitter tomorrow."

Mary drew herself up straight. "You're no needin ta budder him at all," she said. "He kens nothing aboot it. He wis drunk an he canna mind a thing."

Willie came hurriedly to the kitchen door behind Mary. His face was tense.

"Mrs Jamieson," the young policeman began, "let's leave all this till tomorrow, shall we? This isn't the best time …"

"Whatever you want!" said Mary emphatically. "Da moarn, da night, it's aa da sam ta me. I'm just tellin you, you needna spaek ta Donald. It's me you need ta spaek tae. *I* wis drivin da van."

The policeman was silent. He pitied her. Meg pitied her too.

Everybody spoke at once.

Above them all, Mina could be heard saying "Mary! What is du sayin? Du's no needin ta cover up for him ta *yon* extent!"

Mary was unmoved. "It's da truth. I always meant ta tell it if I hed tae, an noo I hae tae. I kent he wis geen ta da pub yon night. I kent he soodna be drivin. I didna want him ta get catched again." Her voice faltered a little, and she turned her eyes to Meg. "I towt, if he lost his licence again, he wid be *sure* ta loss his job." Her lip trembled. "But, so, onywye, I guid ta da pub ta fetch him, an I drave him hame."

Nane o her faimily wis ever supposed ta dö onything wrang.

Willie said, "Mary, naebody ever saw dee at da pub!"

"I never guid in. I kent he wid be mad. I sat in da van till he cam oot. I med sure naebody saw me."

Never laeks admittin tae a faat. Keeps it all quiet.

They were all in the kitchen now, all staring disbelievingly at Mary. She stood small and defiant.

I'm maybe bein ower hard apon her.

Meg said gently, "But Mary, dat doesna mak sense. If du drave da van hame, what cam o dy car?"

"I didna tak my car. I wisna gyaain ta laeve her staandin at da pub for everyeen ta see. I got a taxi. I'll gie you his number if you want. I'll no be gettin him ageen, he wis an awful driver."

Meg's face drained.

"Oh Mary!" she whispered. "What happened?"

The door from the porch opened, and John and Eric came hesitantly in, wet with rain.

"Eric!" came Willie's voice. "Staand still an listen!"

"What happened, Mary?" said Meg.

Mary spoke to Meg. Her eyes became anxious.

"Donald wisna plaesed at I wis dere. But I hed da keys, an he got in. It wis rainin. Aa da idder cars wis geen.

"When we turned in da Whalvoe rodd, it just laid on! Da wipers could hardly tak da watter. I hate drivin yon van, I'm no used wi her. I fin da steerin awful slack."

Eric, right opposite Mary, was ashen white. He sat down on the edge of the kitchen table.

"Eric's car wis parkit abön da Litlagill brig. I noticed her afore, as I cam oot da rodd in da taxi. An as we cam doon for da brig, dey were someen in a yellow jacket at jimpit oot an ran fae ahint Eric's car an seemed ta go right in afore me . . ."

Meg jumped forward and caught Mary, who sobbed into her shoulder. "I tink I hat him! Da van gae a shudder, an I couldna see him ony mair!"

"Du didna mean ta hit him, Mary! It wis an accident!"

Mary raised her head. "Donald wis faan by. I stoppit da van an got oot. He wis lyin doon ower da broo wi his head along a stane. I felt for his pulse — just da wye at Joanne laerned me — an dey were nane." She was trembling. "He wis dead, Meg! Dey were naething I could dö! An it wis rainin. I didna ken wha he wis. An I hed ta get Donald hame! An I wis dat anxious aboot Chris!" She buried her face in Meg's shoulder.

"So, so, Mary. Yon's enough noo. Du's hed a hard time."

"Oh Meg, he wis only twenty-two. I meant ta tell someen, but dey never seemed ta be a chance. Dan I towt at maybe da post-mortem wid shaa at he just fell an hat his head an maybe I hed naething ta dö wi it! An dan *Mam*, an *Donald* . . ."

Doctor Macintyre stepped forward. "Come, come, Mrs Jamieson, that'll do. You've been under a great deal of stress lately. Sit down here. I think when the ambulance comes, I'll send you in with your husband. Let the nurses keep an eye on you tonight. I don't think these gentlemen will require you any further for the moment. They must have heard enough?" He raised a bushy eyebrow towards the two men in uniform.

The kitchen was deathly quiet, apart from Mary's sobbing breathing. The policemen looked at each other.

"I'm sorry," the taller one said. "This has taken me a bit by surprise. We came up from Lerwick at the request of the pub landlord. Then we happened upon the — er — boating accident. If I followed all that correctly, I take it this is the suspected hit-and-run from Friday night?"

Shetland Black

—————— **Chapter 28** ——————

Monday Night

"What does du tink'll happen ta Mary?" Mina asked.

John glanced at his wife, who had been unusually silent since they left Whalvoe. "Weel," he said, "I axed da policemen, when dem an da doctor wis haein yon conflab ida porch. Da spaeky een said at he wisna sure, hit wid be up ta da Fiscal ta decide, but he towt wi da circumstances an her state o mind an aa, hit might even come doon ta careless drivin."

"Wid she hae ta go ta prison?"

"Na, na, I don't tink it."

Mina was thoughtful. "I canna believe aa dis."

"No," said John, turning the corner for home, "you're just blyde ta be hame an oot o it. Wan thing though, it seems ta be brought Willie oot o himsell ageen."

"An Eric is dön weel trow aa dis, poor ting."

"He's turnin oot all right."

"I tink awful ill aboot poor Jack Thompson. Da night at he's pitten in, an haein ta geng hame tae a empty hoose."

"Eric said, if Jack hedna a been dere, Donald wis a goner."

He switched off the engine. There was silence.

"You winder," said Mina, "if Donald really kent what he wis döin."

It was dark.

"Yea," said John. "You winder."

Eric drove the battered Audi back to Roselea. Willie brought Jack in the pick-up.

There was light from car doors, and black shadows on faces.

"Peety aboot dee car," said Willie.

Jack said, "It's only a car."

Eric said, in a rush, "If Donald hedna a hitten dee, du widna a gone efter him, an if du hedna gone efter him, he wid be dead!"

92

Willie said, "Du did a hell of a good job ta get him."

Jack rubbed his bruised face and said wryly, "Dey were a moment when I towt he wis goin ta tak me wi him." He stepped back from the pick-up. "It's been some night," he said.

Willie held out his hand. "Tanks ta dee, boy. Look efter deesell, noo."

Eric handed over the Audi keys, shook Jack's hand, and said, "Du did great."

They watched Jack go into the house of emptiness. They knew what emptiness was.

"Poor bugger," said Willie.

Eric said nothing. But Willie thought there were tears in his eyes.

Jack went in and turned up the heating. Then he went straight to the phone and dialled Scalloway.

"Hello?" It was Marilyn's voice. He suddenly wondered what time it was.

"Marilyn? Is it too late ta phone?"

"Late? Weel, it's eleven o'clock, it's no dat late."

"Is Amy yonder? Is she listenin?"

"She's gone ta bed. What is it, Jack?"

He paused. A cold shiver went through him. He could feel the waves lapping over his head. Feel the rage, feel the panic.

When he felt panic, he lashed out. Sometimes it was the right thing to do. Sometimes it wasn't.

"Marilyn, I'm sorry. I'm *hell* of a sorry! Will du believe me?" He couldn't say another word.

"Jack? Jack, is du OK?"

"No," he managed to say. "I'm no."

They had all gone. There had been nothing but leave-takings since the departure of the ambulance. The police business with Jack, the packing of bags for the hospital, the second round of tea, the piecing together of the stories, it was all finished.

Jack had declared that the damage to his car was a matter for the insurance companies. Though Meg had heard one of the policemen quietly say something about a blood test.

Eric had announced that he had found the böd key inside his car. He'd told his father, and intended to tell the police, first chance he got.

Everyone could then see what must have happened. The Pearson boy had probably sought shelter from the rain in Eric's car, which, as usual, had not been locked. And then, sitting inside the car, a little drunk, a little tired, he had very likely fallen asleep for a while. And, goodness knows, he might have woken up to see lights coming along the road, and got out, intending to flag down the car and ask for a lift, or directions. Maybe he didn't even know where he was. For Jack's sake, nobody, not even Mina, had wondered where he was heading for. Everyone agreed he probably hadn't gone any further than Eric's car.

Well, that all seemed to make reasonable sense. The rest was a tragic accident. They all shook their heads. And now they'd all gone.

"Good neighbours around here. Goodbye, and thank you."

"Meg, I'll be in touch with you once Mary gets home. She may need a bit of help. I think we'll try to persuade Donald into a course of treatment south."

"Guid bliss dee, Meg. What wid she dö athoot dee? Come dee wis, John."

"Thanks for aa dee budder, Meg."

"We'll laeve dee ta lock up dan, Meg. Tanks for everything."

The bathroom floor was dry, the airing-cupboard tidy, the wet towels and blankets removed from the sitting-room, the cups and plates were all dried and put away, the house looked up to Mary's standards. It was half past eleven.

Meg switched off the lights and put the Yale lock on the door.

It was dark, and quiet. A slice of new moon sat uncertainly behind the clouds, shy and solitary. Meg walked carefully home along the road.

Her kitchen light was on. There was a car behind her own. She ran into the house.

Evan was sitting in the armchair, the open Rayburn door blazing warmth. He looked at ease.

"How long are *you* been here?" she demanded, throwing off her jacket.

"Oh, maybe an hour. I was tired of dialling, so I thought I'd come over and see what was going on. And the door was open, of course."

"So you just made yoursell at hame." It felt good to smile.

"Well," he said, "I saw all the cars, and the police car. And then there was an ambulance as well. I just had to wait, didn't I? Too nosey to go home again."

She wanted to keep smiling, keep smiling. She wanted to kiss him.

"So," she said, sitting on his lap, "it's just news at you're efter!"

"No, it isn't," he said.

Shetland Black

―――――――――――― Chapter 29 ――――――――――

Tuesday and Wednesday

On Tuesday, Evan went offshore. He rang the police before he left, also his friend Angus, wrote out an account of the taxi incident on Friday, and left it with Meg.

Willie's collie bitch had five whalps.

Willie reported that Marilyn had been at Roselea. He was sure it was her blonde hair, but he didn't know the car.

Eric, who was excused from work till after the funeral, fed Donald's salmon. He stood for a while in the stern of the boat, looking into the dark water.

The post-mortem result came through, showing evidence of head injury, and also internal injuries consistent with being hit by a moving vehicle. It seemed like old news. The police removed Donald's van for examination. Sergeant Fraser, together with another officer, did another round of visits and statements, briefer this time, except for the long conversation they had with Eric, and the visit to Mary in the hospital.

Mary had slept heavily in the hospital ward, and was kept on medication. Everyone was quite surprised, though relieved, when she was kept in hospital for a second night. Perhaps they would keep her till the funeral was by. Everyone wondered if she realised what Donald had tried to do.

Donald did have a fractured jaw. He seemed totally exhausted and at a very low ebb. He wearily agreed to Doctor Macintyre's suggestion that he should try going away south for a course of treatment. It seemed that it might be possible to go very soon, without going home first. All the better.

No-one had been able to decide, the previous night, who should break the news to Donald and Mary's daughters, but Meg had felt, when Willie asked her, that she could hardly refuse. So by Tuesday evening's visiting hour, she was able to tell Mary that both the lasses would be home as soon as they could. Joanne would drive up to join Chris and fly from Aberdeen. Meg did not add that Chris seemed unsure whether she

96

would go back again. Both daughters had been amazed, as well as shocked. Mary had obviously kept everything from them for a long time.

On her way home from the hospital, Meg found two shaken-looking young New Zealanders standing disconsolate at the loch of Litlagill. They were very glad to talk.

"What to hell was Terry doin here?" they wondered. "He must a bin lost. Nevah did hev much sense o direction."

Meg resolved to repeat that remark, and agreed that he must have been lost.

They were young and cold and shocked. Meg took them home and made them food. Heard about Terry, his family and theirs. And by and by, she told them almost all the story, as far as she knew it.

Then Wednesday came, and everyone's thoughts turned back to Cissie.

It was a cold, dry day, perfectly calm, as Cissie was laid to rest in her husband's grave in the Brugafirth kirkyard by the sea. A black crowd of people followed her solemnly to the grave.

Eric walked steady and straight and carried the coffin carefully. It said "Christina Mary Hendry, 75 years", but he knew it was only a body inside. The kind words of the minister in the kirk, the thoughts and the memories of Granny, these things had moved him. Not the coffin, not the hole in the ground. This was a task to be done, and he did it properly, carefully.

Clivagarth, that's where you missed Granny. Not here. You felt it at Clivagarth. Just the *absence.*

He stood by Willie and John as the funeral company moved forward to shake their hands. A lot of folk, he thought. So many older folk he didn't know.

There weren't many women, apart from Meg and Mina and Gail. Cissie's particular friends were older women, who rarely went to funerals. Cissie, he knew, had never been to one, not even her own husband's. He couldn't imagine why. Some kind of tradition.

Jack Thompson, coming along the line, warmly shook hands with Willie and Eric. He had a proper black eye, which nobody mentioned. By now, probably half the north mainland knew how he had got it.

Nobody asked where Donald was either.

Behind the crowd, at the kirkyard gate, wearing a black coat and a grey headscarf, stood Marilyn, waiting. She must be waiting for Jack.

It was understood that pall-bearers and family members would return to Clivagarth. Willie and Eric had spent the morning tidying up. The minister was invited too. Cissie had liked the minister; Willie liked him too, and felt guilty that he had been so hard to find at home for the past two days. The man had had to arrange the details of the funeral service with Mina.

"Jack," Willie said, "du'll come doon alang da hoose efter. We're gyaain ta hae tay, an a gless o somethin afore da folk gengs hame." Willie would never have seen Marilyn. John and Eric said in unison, "Tak Marilyn."

Jack looked surprised, hesitated, then nodded.

Eric wondered what sort of gathering it would be. He hadn't been able to face them all the last time, had fled straight to his room. He imagined Granny would have taken charge. Today, he and Willie had bargained that they would not allow Mina to take charge. They were first at the house, and had the tea in the pots, the sandwiches and things all on the table, when Mina and John arrived.

"Oh!" she said, looking around. "My, you are da efficient!"

Willie winked.

And it turned out all right really, just folk you knew and were glad to see, and who really knew Granny. Except Jack, and he was fine, and Marilyn.

Marilyn seemed a bit shy at first, but she sat and talked to Mina, and then she talked to Meg, and she talked to Gail for ages.

The conversation inevitably turned at last to the events of the weekend, to Mary and to Donald, and to what would become of them.

One of the cousins said to Jack, "An it wis dee at saved his life?"

Jack looked ill at ease, but said yes. "Poor Donald."

Marilyn was looking at her husband.

"Jack wis great!" said Eric loudly.

Jack shrugged. "I can sweem. An when someen hits me, I — er — I usually hit back." He looked down.

Marilyn was still looking at him. Then she looked down too.

A few minutes later, Mina and Gail went to the sink to wash up. Willie looked across at Eric and said, "Eric, maybe Marilyn wid laek ta see da whalps?"

Aboot time, Dad.

He rose. "Wid du?"

"Oh yes. How many do you hae?" She got to her feet, smiling, and followed him out the door.

The whalps were in the barn, in a peerie hay-filled enclosure, nuzzling up to their mother. Eric and Marilyn leaned on the rail and looked.

"Well," said Marilyn, "how is things, Eric?"

"Aa right." He looked down at the wriggling warm black and white mass, not at her. "I wanted ta tell dee, it's aa right. Da key o da böd wis in my car, an I'm said dat, an I'm said whan I cam back ta da car. Dan I said I wisna wantin folk ta ken whaar I wis been, an dey said, weel, I might hae ta spaek ta da Fiscal, but dey didna tink at onybody needed ta ken dat, because it doesna maitter noo."

"Thanks."

"It's been *awful*."

"I ken."

There was a pause, then Marilyn said hesitantly, "When du guid back ta dy car — wis he dere dan? Did du fin him?"

"I fan him. I couldna miss him, walkin oot da rodd wi a torch in me haand. He wis dead. I kent dat."

"Du most a gotten some gluff."

"No half! I kent I sood a reported it, but — weel . . ." He gave her a quick sideways look. "Weel, what could I say aboot whaar I wis been? An dan I towt dey might blame me for it if I couldna say whaar I wis been. An when I fan da key, it gluffed da shit oot o me! I aye meant ta say I wis run oot o petrol at da loch onywye, if onybody axed aboot da car staandin yonder, an I stack ta dat. But I made up a great story aboot whaar I wis been efter dat, an got Hamish an Derek draggit intil it ta back me up. Never said aboot da key, denied I wis ever seen onything." He felt ashamed, pitiful.

"Poor Eric," said Marilyn softly.

He looked at her again. "Du's no telled Jack?"

She shook her head. "Du most be jokin! An him dat sorry for no trustin me!"

Silence.

"It wis awful silly o me ta come alang dee."

"It wis awful silly o me ta invite dee. I dönna tink I realised . . ."

". . . how much I fancied dee? I still do, but dat's it. I'll never do anything laek yon again. Aa yon lyin! An I wid hate ta do anything ta hurt Jack. Or dee."

He faced her. "Are you back tagidder?"

"Weel . . ."

"You ought ta be! He's a good guy! An he needs dee. I dönna want ta spend da rest o me life feelin guilty aboot you."

At the base of her throat the skin was soft, and so fine. Eric remembered, and blushed.

"Pit Friday night oot o dee mind," he said. "I tink du soodna fin it hard ta forget aboot!" He turned his head away.

He felt her hand on his shoulder. "Dönna pit deesell doon. I wis flattered, an dat's da truth. But it wis aa wrang. I widna do it again."

They walked back to the house. Meg was on her way out.

"Cheerio, bairns," she said. "I'll hae ta geng an feed da public!"

Cissie's windows looked across at them blankly.

"Oh less!" said Meg. "Der naethin sae sad as an empty hoose."

Marilyn went inside.

Eric went to see if any of the cars needed moving out of Meg's way. He was glad of a moment to himself.

Shetland Black

─────────────── **Chapter 30** ───────────────

Christmas

The letter was addressed to Mrs Meg Inkster, The Shop, Brugafirth, Shetland. It lay among a bundle of what Meg took to be Christmas cards, until mid-morning when she at last had time to open her mail. Friday was the busiest day of the week.

It was an air-mail letter from New Zealand. Meg read it through twice.

Dear Mrs Inkster,

You will be surprised to receive a letter from me, but I hope that you may be able to help me. My name is Pauline Roberts, and I am a hospital nursing sister. I am married, with two daughters, one 26, the other 20. My father came from Shetland, and I am very interested in tracing my family tree, but could never get much information out of him, not even a place-name. He died two years ago, and in his old age was very forgetful.

My younger daughter is at college in Wellington, and last weekend she brought home her new boyfriend to visit us. He seems a nice boy — I believe you have met him. His name is Ryan Armstrong, and he visited Scotland and Shetland earlier this year, in rather sad circumstances.

He told us the story about his friend, Terry Pearson, and I was particularly excited to hear how the old lady had thought he might be related to her, and how her brother was called Davie Pearson.

My father's name was David Pearson. He was born on 4th January, 1910, and arrived in this country, I think, about 1930. He was always vague about the date.

He told us many years ago that when he was a young man, he got into a fight in a dockside pub in Wellington and accidentally killed someone. After that, he spent some years in prison.

He never talked about his home, it seemed to hurt him to do so. We used to think that he must have been unhappy at home. I now believe he was ashamed of himself, and for this reason never sought to make contact, and always felt guilty.

I remember him as a gentle, rather melancholy man. He always hated violence, and never touched drink again in his life.

I am so sure I have found the family, I hate to think I might be wrong! Please can you send more information, and/or put me in touch with any members of the Pearson family.

We are all waiting on tenterhooks — my two brothers, myself and our families. Please reply as soon as possible. Thank you very much.

Yours sincerely,

Pauline Roberts (née Pearson)

Meg gazed at the thin blue page. "Oh, Cissie!" she said aloud.

After a moment, she lifted the phone.

"Willie? No, Eric? I never kent du wis hame!"

"Just come dis moarnin — hi, Meg!"

"Well, now, how's du laekin Edinburgh?"

"Fine. Splendid. But it's fine ta be hame."

"Du'll no be seen dee new nephew yet?"

"No, but Gail is takkin him ower dis efternön. I'm seen Chris's peerie lass, though. It's kinda lightsome haein dem in Granny's hoose."

"Is dee faider aboot?"

"He's feedin sheep, as du might ken. Him an Donald. Donald is surely doin no too bad."

"Winderful, so far. Mary is kinda up an doon. Chris keeps an eye on her, though. Jack an Marilyn moved ta Lerook, but of coorse, du wid ken dat."

"I heard, yes."

"Dey're fine, though. An it's no sae lonely for her."

"An what's all doin wi dee, Meg?"

"Oh, just much da sam as ever, Eric. Wirkin awa. No changes."

Meg looked at the cheeky birthday card from Evan, still pinned on her office wall. There were decisions to be made shortly.

"Weel, onywye, Eric," she said, "come ower ta da shop as shön as du can, an tak dee faider wi dee. I hae somethin ta shaa you."